Jiggles and the Archaeologists

Jiggles, Volume 2

Mary Tales

Published by Mary Tales Books, 2017.

This is a work of fiction. Similarities to real people, places, or events are entirely coincidental.

JIGGLES AND THE ARCHAEOLOGISTS

First edition. August 6, 2017.

Copyright © 2017 Mary Tales.

ISBN: 979-8227418623

Written by Mary Tales.

Part 1

The airstrip was a scar on the pale desert, the edges indistinct where small fingers of sand had blown onto it.

The twin engined Hawker "Hooligan" biplane circled the strip, and the camp and dig it serviced, before lining up to land. Sand eddying across the dunes allowed the pilot to judge wind direction and speed so she could make a perfect smooth landing. It was only when the full weight of the aeroplane had settled on the wheels that the rough nature of the surface became apparent and the cabin began to shake.

Veronica Jiggleswick- Ronny to her family and Jiggles to her friends- was the pilot. In the co-pilot's seat was her old school chum Ally. Ally had shuffled forward to perch on the edge of her seat, a far away look on her face as the rumble excited her sensitive parts. She pouted as the aeroplane slowed and taxied off the end of the runway.

When the aeroplane had come to a halt, the first person out of the enclosed cabin was Ginge, Jiggleswick Air's mechanic. He put chocks under the Hooligan's wheels and did a quick walk around to check for damage. Satisfied all was well he opened the luggage compartment and pulled out a small metal step so the passengers could alight.

As Ginge dealt with the luggage, Jiggles and Ally ran their own post flight checks. Jiggles told herself she could relax now. She had been tense for the whole of the last leg of their journey from England to Egypt. They had planned their crossing of the Mediterranean where it narrowed at its Eastern end. It was a relatively safe and easy jaunt, but Jiggles couldn't help but remember that her brother had disappeared several years earlier whilst flying over the same sea. Ally could see all these thoughts on her friend's face, so she suggested, "Come on, let's have a look around."

Their passengers were milling around the luggage, uncertain of what to do or where to go. Leader of the group was Professor Horatio Quince. He was an eminent Egyptologist, though his reputation had been somewhat tarnished by his part in a recent country house murder. With him was his assistant Eustace, a weedy tweedy undergraduate from Magdalen and a good family. The final member of the group was Fiona Smythe-Whyte, the professor's secretary and illustrator. Fiona was the classic English rose- tall, willowy and pale with ice blue eyes and thick auburn hair. Jiggles and Ally- and even Ginge, who was more interested in the boys- had spent the whole journey through Europe hoping for a glimpse of Fiona unbuttoned- literally or metaphorically- but she was disappointingly old fashioned. Fiona's dress sense was at least a decade out of date, and demure to a fault. Ally, whose family had made its fortune in the rag trade, took Fiona's refusal to flatter her natural assets with a sympathetic cut as a nearly personal insult. She had made a vow to get the rose to bloom if at all possible.

For now the question was what should they do next? Professor Quince was joining the dig on a famously lost 'pyramid' (actually a large underground tomb complex and the town which serviced it) and expected to be met as soon as the aeroplane landed. However, only now was there any sign of movement from the camp. A group of local workers in dusty white clothes were walking rapidly toward them. "Natives." announced Eustace dismissively.

"Swarthy." sighed Ally and Ginge in unison.

As the crowd drew closer a westerner pushed through to the front. Not that tall, he was well built, with a handsome square face atop broad shoulders. He wore a suit and a wide brimmed hat to shade his bespectacled eyes. As he stepped up to the newcomers he removed the glasses and put them in his breast pocket. He held out a strong calloused hand, "Professor Quince, I presume." Jiggles recognised his accent as American, but couldn't pinpoint which state.

"And who are you?"

"Montana Smith, Professor. I'm the chief archaeologist on the dig." Quince winced when he took Montana's hand. Whilst the professor had soft, plump academic's hands, Smith's were rough and strong. He was obviously a hands-on archaeologist, more than willing to join in with the digging. Quince, by contrast, was at home in the sheltered halls of his college, looking over artefacts after they had been cleaned and catalogued. Now that Jiggles gave him a closer look it was clear that Montana was uncomfortable in his suit. It wasn't the discomfort Quince, Eustace and Fiona were displaying- being far too hot because they wore too many layers. Rather, Smith didn't like the formality implied by his current attire, and would prefer to be in work wear. Jiggles decided she liked him.

"You were the chief archaeologist." Quince announced, "You do understand that I am here to take over from you and see that finds are documented properly."

"I was aware of this, yes." Montana kept most of the edge out of his voice. "If you'll come down to the dig I can get you up to date on our progress.

"Yes, yes. But first I want to see our quarters. I need to freshen up."

As Montana turned away to start giving orders Ginge chipped in, "I really need to get the kite squared away. Could you spare a few of your chaps to help?"

"Of course." Montana turned to one of the workers who was older and better dressed. They conversed in a mixture of English and the local dialect then the team boss started issuing orders. A small group gathered around Ginge, smiling and eager to learn what they had to do with his exotic piece of machinery. The rest picked up bags and set off down the track to the camp.

"We shall get your stuff into a tent or whatever and meet you down there." Jiggles told Ginge. He nodded and immediately set about issuing orders to his ragtag ground crew.

* * *

Quince fussed and fretted over his quarters and showed every indication that he planned to spend an absolute age unpacking. Jiggles and Ally took the time he gave them to start work on Fiona.

On the journey down they had stayed in hotels on their stopovers, with separate rooms. Now, however, they would be sharing a tent, and canvas made sneaky peeks much simpler. Jiggles and Ally didn't need to discuss their plans-they would tease the girl a little, to see if she showed any proclivities for tribadism, and if she did Ally would introduce her to its joys.

The tent was large, with an oblong footprint and two poles holding up the roof. A wall of canvas hung from the roof, splitting the interior into a communal area with a small space for ablutions by the entry flaps and three little bedrooms. The bedrooms, large enough for a camp bed and clothes trunk, were also separated by hanging canvas walls. In the right light these walls would be almost see through. Jiggles and Ally chose the rooms either side of Fiona, and hoped she would have her lamp on when she dis-robed.

There was an enamelled bowl on a folding table in the ablutions area with a pile of white cotton towels beside it. Under the table was a large jug full of water, from which Jiggles half filled the bowl. She and Ally stripped off their blouses and brassieres and dipped towels in the water to start washing. Fiona, who had been in her bedroom checking her trunk, returned just in time to see the friends cleaning themselves. She stopped short and made a shocked squeak.

Jiggles and Ally turned toward Fiona, pretending to be surprised by her cry. Doing so, they presented her with two pairs of breasts, each magnificent in their own way. Jiggles chest was firm and full, with hardening nipples tilted up to the ceiling, Ally's breasts were smaller, almost perfect hemispheres. Fiona, reddening and making little flustered noises, couldn't keep her eyes from flicking back and forth between the orbs. Jiggles and Ally, almost in unison, looked down and feigned surprise at the sight of their own nakedness. "Oh. Oh, sorry." said Jiggles as she and Ally covered their nipples. "We're just so used to our own company that it feels natural to be naked around each other."

"We didn't mean to make you uncomfortable. We just forgot you were here." While she had been saying these reassuring words Ally had let her arm drop, revealing herself again, and had been moving toward Fiona. She reached back and took a damp towel from Jiggles, then offered it to Fiona. "You look awfully hot. Here, take this and dab your forehead with it. That will cool you down, and then you should wash. It gets terribly sweaty in the confines of an aeroplane cabin and you must want to freshen up."

As Fiona buried her face in the towel Ally turned to Jiggles with a grin. Jiggles gave her a nod, they might be in with a chance with Fiona. They wouldn't push her any farther than she wanted to go, but hopefully that would be a long way. Ally would make most of the running, she was, after all, the one most interested in women. Jiggles might join in, but she had her eyes on the enigmatic young archaeologist who had greeted them.

Fiona dabbed her forehead with the towel. "That is better. Oh, erm." For a moment she stared at Ally's breasts. Her right hand faltered after it handed back the towel, and looked like it might drop to the swelling bosom. She snatched it back and clasped her left hand, arms shielding her own, clothed, breasts.

"I do hope you don't find our behaviour too indecorous." Ally apologised. "We are going to be sharing this tent for the next few weeks, I do hope we can get along. Jiggles and I are a little more open than most, but we would not want to alienate you, so we can cover up if you want."

Fiona looked from Jiggles to Ally- at their faces and then their exposed breasts- then back again. "Oh,no, don't do that on my account. Perhaps I should be somewhat more open myself. But, well, not just yet. I shall go and change into something lighter in, erm, here." Fiona stepped into her bedroom partition and closed the flap.

The outside wall of the bedrooms faced west and this late in the day a strong bright light shone on it. This cast the shadow Jiggles and Ally had hoped for on the door of Fiona's bedroom. They finished undressing as she started, casting occasional glances at her silhouette. First she struggled out of her dress, then started on her under-things. They were obviously restricting, and involved a multitude of knots. Eventually she was naked, and they watched her outline stretch and turn. She was a tall slip of a girl, with the slightest of waists and small, almost conical breasts. They watched as she looked down at the breasts and cupped them in her hands. Then she ran her hands down her stomach, over the slight bulge of her pubic bone and between her legs.

Fiona opened the flap to her bedroom just enough to poke her head through it. She had let her hair down and it framed her face with tight curls. She looked gorgeous and the smile when she found Jiggles and Ally were naked melted their hearts whilst warming them lower down. "Would you be able to bring the washing bowl over?" she asked.

"Come now Fiona, let's all be girls together." teased Ally, "We know you have nothing to be ashamed of."

Fiona was confused, but not stupid. It took her but a moment to realise where the sun was and how she had put on a shadow show for her tent mates. She blushed a most delightful shade of red and bit her lip, but started untying the flap all the same. As each tie came away she struggled to grasp the flap about her modesty. It only just worked.

Jiggles and Ally smiled invitingly at Fiona. Slowly, enticingly, the flap moved aside. The body they had just seen in silhouette was revealed in all its alabaster glory. Her breasts were indeed lovely pert cones with deep red nipples and areolae. She had a boyish waist and a flat stomach which tapered down to a luscious deep brown pubic bush and orchid like vulva lips.

Fiona looked from Jiggles to Ally then cast her embarrassed stare down to the floor. "I must seem so plain to you. You are both so gorgeous."

"So are you my dear." Ally announced as she and Jiggles moved either side of Fiona. They each ran fingers over the nearest of Fiona's breasts, tweaking the nipples and raising a squeak. Without a doubt they had found a potential playmate. Ally took a towel from the pile, "Let me wash those for you." she offered, dipping the towel in the bowl then wringing a little of the water out.

"Well, I, erm, I.... Okay." Fiona's hands had been flitting around as she fought her shyness and the prudishness she had been brought up with. Now that she had made her decision she clasped them behind her back, causing her breasts to thrust out.

Ally gave Jiggles a look that was easy to read. She was in love- or at the very least, lust- could she please, please, please get first pass at Fiona. Jiggles smiled and gave her a little nod, stepping back as she did. Fiona didn't notice. Her gaze was fixed on the towel in Ally's hand, waiting for it to touch her skin. As it drew closer still she closed her eyes and threw her head back, offering up her throat. Ally gently stroked the towel down Fiona's neck and between her breasts.

Fiona was trembling, and her breath came in little gasps. Jiggles was turned on just watching, she wanted to reach between her legs and gently play with her wet lower lips. Heaven only knew how turned on Ally must be.

Ally ran the towel under one breast and then the other. Fiona practically purred, arching her back to offer the gorgeous cones of her breasts up for a more thorough cleaning. Ally teased the nipples ever stiffer. Then she had an idea. Wetting the towel again, she held it just over the base of Fiona's neck and squeezed a big drop of water from it. The droplet zigzagged down the valley between Fiona's breasts then undulated over her ribs and onto her belly. It slowed a little as it left a damp trail on the girl's skin, then poised on the rim of her oval belly button.

"Ladies!" Quince's voice rang out.

Fiona squealed. Her hands whipped around to cover her breasts and pubic area. She almost doubled over trying to cover up.

Jiggles and Ally looked around. Quince's voice had been so clear it had been like he were in the tent with them. "Ladies?" he repeated, and they realised he was standing right outside the tent, beside the closed flap. "Is anything wrong?"

"We were just washing. The water is a little cold." Jiggles decided to mix the truth with a realistic lie. When she and Ally looked around again Fiona had disappeared and the flap to her bedroom was being hurriedly tied up again.

"Are you decent?"

"No. No, we're not. But we shall be dressed again in ten minutes or so."

"Oh, well, I suppose we can wait that long. Meet me in the office tent and we shall go down to the dig site for a quick look around." This time, not distracted by a naked rose, they could distinctly hear his feet crunching on the fine gravel path. Jiggles and Ally shared a sad look then retired to their bedrooms to change.

* * *

Fiona had wrapped herself in what looked like a sack with a pretty pale floral pattern printed on it. She rushed out of the tent without so much as a glance at either Jiggles or Ally and walked ahead of them all the way.

The site, and the areas around it, was dusty and open. It was possible to walk from one place to another by whichever route was most direct, yet an ordered series of paths had grown up, paler scars in the dust showing the way. Rather than chaos the camp had streets.

There was a slight incline down to the main dig. Three large square holes were surrounded by trenches going off in all directions following features of interest or just exploring the buried ruins. Most of the workers were busy with the largest of the holes, but others moved to and fro or dug elsewhere.

The site's office tent, to the North and uphill of the holes and trenches, was almost twice the size of the accommodation ones, open on two sides and half filled with four rows of tables. On these tables were arrayed various items from the dig- pottery shards, utensils, blades and other bits and pieces. Everything was being documented by workers and students. Compared to the bustle and noise of the dig outside this was surprisingly quiet. The other half of the tent was given over to a large table with maps and paperwork on it. Quince, Ginge and Eustace stood beside it, being shown documents by Montana Smith. They looked up as Jiggles, Ally and Fiona arrived. "Ah, ladies, so good of you to join us." Quince announced, "Doctor Smith was just showing us the map of the valley and where else he wanted to dig."

"There are claims of other tombs in the valley, but everything we know about their location is based upon rumour. We need to find out more before we send survey teams out for a closer look at any of them."

"Which is why," Quince puffed up with importance as he made his announcement, "I have retained the services of Jiggleswick Air. In the last war I worked on aerial reconnaissance. It is quite incredible what you can see when you look down upon the battlefield from an aeroplane. I thought it would be awfully clever to apply that principle to surveying archaeological sites."

Montana, Jiggles, Ally and Ginge all considered this idea before the American archaeologist announced, "Y'know I believe that may just work." He studied the map then looked from it to Jiggles, "How much ground can you cover in one flight?"

Jiggles leant over the map, close to Montana, and went over it with him. "That depends upon how high you want me to fly. Too high or too low and you may miss details." She checked the scale. "But we should be able to cover all of this in a few days once we get started. Perhaps we can take a test flight tomorrow and we can work out the optimum height?"

"It would be a pleasure ma'am."

"Very good." huffed Quince, "I had Eustace arrange delivery of sufficient fuel for the aircraft."

"They tell me it has already arrived. Of course, I shall have to check that the locals have it stored correctly." Eustace announced. Ally had the impression he was giving her and Fiona a judging look, like he knew what they had been doing in the tent and did not approve.

Montana circled a few places of interest on the map. "Maybe we can discuss this in detail later." he suggested to Jiggles.

"That sounds like a spiffing idea." she replied.

"Yes. Yes. Very good." Quince harrumphed, "But perhaps now we can take a look at the workings."

"Of course." Montana took a battered old leather hat from one of the seats. He just had to drop it onto his head and it sat perfectly in place. It obviously belonged there, though it didn't go with the suit Montana wore. Perhaps there was a whole battered and worn outfit which fitted him like a second skin.

Jiggles would like to see him in that outfit- much more comfortable and relaxed- almost as much as she wanted to see him out of it.

Leading the way to the largest of the holes, Montana described various aspects for the benefit of the non archaeologists. "We've started calling this the Valley Of The Wizards. It roughly equates to some of the local names for it, and it has a nice ring to it. The whole valley is an artificial flood plain. We don't understand why yet, but the ancient inhabitants built a series of dams to redirect the seasonal river which ran through here, making it meander over the whole valley and slowly silt it up. It looks like the tombs and temples, or at least this one, were sealed up and buried before the flooding began. Unlike the Pharaohs who built the pyramids as ostentatious reminders of their power, it's as if the rulers of this area, or their subjects, wanted to be hidden from history."

"There are rumours of objects with great occult powers in the burial chambers." Eustace interjected, drawing a disdainful look from Quince and a shrug from Montana.

"Nobody believes that superstitious claptrap, of course." Quince commented, "Do carry on Doctor Smith."

"The river has long since changed its course and the valley became barren hundreds, if not thousands, of years ago. Since then there have only been the occasional nomads and outcasts passing through. It seems that even the grave robbers have missed this valley. This site was uncovered by wind erosion clearing the sand from atop the ruins. One particular trader used it as a way point on his route and eventually news of it reached the university in Cairo, and then me and Professor Quince. Of course, as soon as we started digging we began to hear all the ghost stories and legends."

"About objects of great arcane power?" Jiggles enquired cheekily.

"And some very.... interesting ceremonies, involving ritual deflowering of virgins by the priests." Fiona let out something part way between a squeak and a cough at the thought of this. When she realised that Jiggles and Ally were looking at her she went bright red again. "Not virgin sacrifices though, not in the way the pulps would have them, anyway." Montana continued, "The stories are very specific on this. There seems to have been a whole culture of sex rites which are going to be fascinating to find out about." Montana, too, had noticed Fiona's flush and, evilly, was doing his own bit to make it hotter. "Ah, here we are. Let's go down shall we." he motioned to a ladder down into the largest hole.

They climbed down the ladder to a rickety scaffolding balcony and then down again to the current level of the workings. A smaller hole within the hole was the focus of activity. Dusty earth was being passed up from this hole in baskets then sifted for shards. When it was judged to no longer hold anything which might be historically significant the earth was shovelled into another basket and lifted from the hole. "Very thorough." Quince commented approvingly.

"We do our best. Amid!" Montana shouted over the sounds of work. "How are things going?"

A darkly handsome young man separated himself from the activity and headed towards them. "Very good Doctor Smith." he announced as he slapped dust from his hands and sleeves. He was tall and slim and managed to make his plain work clothes look tailored and stylish. He had the bearing of a prince, Ginge thought when he had recovered from his initial swoon. "It looks like you were correct." the dusty vision announced, "This could easily be the roof to a chamber. And we think there is an air gap beneath it."

"It seems you timed your arrival perfectly Professor." Montana said to Quince. "This is Amid. He's my star pupil and the informal foreman. He tells me that his father, grandfather and several generations before them were grave robbers, but his mother wanted him to go legit."

"Before they robbed the graves my family was in them. You missed out the part about being able to trace my line back to some of Egypt's oldest royal families, Doctor Smith. Would our guests like to come down and have a look?"

They descended another, shorter, ladder as the workers crowded back from the middle of the hole.

They had uncovered a section of neatly cut stone which showed a clean, straight edge where it butted up against another section. "We have cleaned out some of the seam and it appears they join with what you described as 'tongue and groove'. If you look down here," Amid pointed at a section of the stone which had only just been uncovered and was still dusty, "you can see hieroglyphs. We think that when we have uncovered and translated those, we will know how to get in."

"Couldn't you just blast an opening in here? In this stone you've already uncovered?" asked Eustace.

This suggestion drew disapproving looks from Quince, Montana, Amid and Fiona. Jiggles, Ally and Ginge weren't sure just how bad an idea the proposed vandalism was judged to be, so they resisted the urge to join in the glare.

"If we can find the correct way in we can explore the complex properly." Amid explained slowly, "We can document it correctly and learn more about its function. If we damage the roof too much we risk the whole structure collapsing, destroying fragile artefacts and compromising the whole dig. Patience is a virtue. It has been down there for millennia, a few more days should make little difference." Amid shaded his eyes and checked the angle of the sun. "It is almost the end of the shift and all the work for the day. If you do not mind I shall get the safety barriers erected and see the crew off."

As Amid set about giving the workers orders the academics and their pilots headed for the ladders. "Grave robbers, you say?" commented Quince.

"And royalty?" added Ginge.

"Well, it could all be a bit of colour." conceded Montana, "But Amid did know a lot about ancient history and the construction of tombs even before he started studying under me. After you, Miss Jiggleswick." Montana let Jiggles mount the ladder ahead of him then followed close behind, studying what was above him intently as he went. Ally paid close attention to this trick, and pulled her own version on Fiona. When she looked up she could see past Fiona's sensible shoes all the way up to some surprisingly skimpy cami-knickers. She smiled and revelled in the roll of the girl's round buttocks in the close fitting material.

When they were all at the top of the hole again, Montana announced, "There is a communal meal every evening for the students and foremen when you're all ready."

"Eustace and I have to go over all your documentation. Have some food sent to our tent." replied Quince.

"Okay. Ladies? Mister Ginge?" Montana's question received nods all round. "Okay, well, let's meet at the food tent in about two hours."

* * *

Ginge had not studied his tent when he first arrived, simply dropping his bags in it and rushing out to look around the site. Now he had time to check it out properly.

If he had seen the girls' tent he would have seen that his was smaller. However, it was also only a two person tent, the bedrooms being partitions in the rear half. The rest of the tent was furnished with rugs and cushions, but for the corner with the washing bowl on a table which had reed mats under it.

There was a polished metal mirror behind the wash basin. Ginge checked his reflection in it and realised he was bright red. He always forgot how quickly his pale skin burnt in strong sunlight and now his head and neck down to his opened collar were going to be tender. He could feel the heat from the skin already, and winced at the thought of the coming tenderness. Beside the wash basin were bottles of oils, possibly intended to moisturise tender skin. Ginge decided to try them out.

Carefully and slowly Ginge unbuttoned his shirt and dropped it to the floor. He kicked off his shoes and removed his trousers and jockey shorts. He filled the washing bowl from the jug under the table and started washing his hands and arms. There was a smaller jug behind the bowl, so he used this to rinse his arms and upper body- trying to get the water to dribble back into the bowl.

Ginge was pondering the best way to wash his chest and lower body without soaking the floor when a voice behind him said, "Ah, hello mister Ginge."

Ginge looked around to see Amid tying the tent flaps together. The other man's smile became an expression of concern as his eyes became used to the light and he spotted Ginge's burnt face and neck. He hurried over, "Oh dear, oh dear. You have had too much sun."

Ginge shrugged, "I should have known better."

"You Europeans burn so easily, particularly copper heads such as you." Amid had been tracing the edges of Ginge's red skin, without touching it, but got distracted by the freckles on his hairless arm and ran a finger over them. "You have these, what are these little brown marks on your skin called?"

"Freckles."

"Freckles. All the people I have ever met with freckles have not coped so very well in the sunshine. You need to stay shaded as much as you can." Amid was checking out the whole of Ginge's body, spotting freckles on his back and down to his tight buttocks. Always a fan of attention from a handsome man (or attractive woman if he was honest), Ginge found the it perked up his penis. Commonly known as little Ginge, the organ was becoming plumper and harder and rising. By the time Amid moved around to see it, little Ginge was pointing straight forward at the wash basin. "Oh my." ejaculated Amid, "Does this magnificent beast have freckles?"

"I don't know, I've never looked."

Amid dropped to his knees immediately. He took little Ginge between thumb and forefinger and moved it side to side as he examined it. "Oh yes. There is one there, and a little cluster of them here. And there are more here." All the while that Amid was looking at the penis pointing out freckles the organ grew ever harder, until it was pointing straight up. Eventually Amid reached the tip and exclaimed excitedly, "Oh! You still have your sheath!"

"My...?"

Amid manipulated little Ginge until he had tugged the foreskin over the bulbous dark red head. He pointed at it, "This. Your, er...."

"Oh, my foreskin!" pronounced Ginge, a touch breathless from Amid's handling.

"Yes. I had mine removed when I was very young. We all do it."

"You know, I have never seen that." Ginge lied. He had learnt a long time ago that the occasional untruth would help him into other men's pants.

Amid stood. "I can show you." He was keen to enlighten Ginge, if the front of his trousers were anything to go by. His shirt and trousers were quickly discarded and he soon stood before Ginge in naked glory and stiffening nicely. It was a magnificent erection, every bit as dark and regal looking as its owner and it bobbed and waved as Amid stepped forward.

"That is lovely isn't it?" Ginge marvelled as little Ginge nudged up against his new friend. He reached down and stroked the two of them together, pressing them against each other. Amid's cock was warm and smooth and the feeling as its head rubbed against his was exquisite. He had to take a closer look.

Ginge was on his knees in an instant, just as keen as Amid had been to get a look at a new penis. It wasn't the largest he had ever seen, that honour belonged to an usher he had met in a cinema near Leicester Square, but it was one of the top ten. Ginge paused for a moment, to muse that he had seen an awful lot of penises in his time. He smiled. Amid was looking down at him, wondering at the delay. Best not to keep his graciously endowed host waiting any longer.

The skin of Amid's cock was darker than any Ginge had ever licked before. This didn't bother him- it tasted the same and felt just as exquisite. He flicked his tongue around the edge of Amid's cock head, eliciting a happy moan, then he licked down the shaft to the balls. Cupping them in his hand, he lifted them to his lips and half sucked each into his mouth. Next, he nibbled up Amid's shaft with his lips. He stopped just before taking the head of Amid's erection between his lips, teasing.

"You are more open than the other Western men I have met." Amid announced, his hips swaying and teasing his glans toward Ginge's mouth.

"Really?"

"Oh Professor Smith is a fine man, I admire him immensely, but he is all for the ladies. And all of the English academics and students, well, I think they sleep with all the buttons on their shirts fastened up."

"Gosh, that is a shame. And a surprise. Some of my finest bouts have been with chaps from Oxford and Cambridge."

"Maybe I should try harder. But I must say, I knew as soon as I saw you in the trench that you would enjoy this. That was why I was not so upset at no longer having a tent to myself."

Ginge smiled. Then he opened his mouth wide and swallowed as much as he could of Amid's magnificent cock. Amid had not been expecting this and yelped, mostly in pleasure. Ginge slurped his way back up it, releasing it with a theatrical slobber. Then he just as quickly swallowed it again. "Oh my." ejaculated Amid.

Ginge repeated his swallowing trick a few more times before sucking hard on the head as his tongue played around it. Amid's thighs were quivering and his penis was beginning to twitch. Ginge took it out of his mouth and began working on it with his hand- two quick strokes then one slow, repeating the rhythm as Amid drew ever closer to orgasm.

"It. Has. Been. Some. Time." Amid gasped out as he spurted semen over Ginge's face and chest. "I apologise for being so quick."

"There's no need to apologise when you're carrying around something like this." Ginge reassured Amid. He squeezed the still hard erection, coaxing a drop of semen out and licking it from the tip, which drew a hiss of pleasure from Amid.

"I will wash you." Amid offered, "And I have oils which will sooth the burning of your skin. Then perhaps we should do something with your own magnificent, freckled beast."

* * *

Both Jiggles and Ally recognised the satisfied grin Ginge sported when he entered the dining tent. He sat opposite them at the long table, favouring a still sensitive groin as he stepped over the bench seat. The three of them had one of their coded silent conversations- all glances and barely perceptible nods- as they tried to extract information from him. There was no need, as it became obvious soon enough where Ginge had been getting some.

Amid entered the dining tent carrying a hat. It was white and round, with a peak at the front to shade the eyes and a cape of sorts hanging down from it for most of its circumference to protect the back and sides of the neck from the sun. "I think this shall protect your sensitive skin." he suggested as he handed it to Ginge. "And if you keep using the oils I showed you to keep your skin from drying up."

"Thanks old chap." Ginge tried the hat on. "What do you think girls?"

"You look like you have just joined the Foreign Legion." Ally opined.

"Yet I have so little I want to forget." Ginge announced with a sideways glance at Amid that confirmed everything.

There were three tables in the dining tent, but Fiona had picked the seat next to Ally. Still, she couldn't bring herself to cast more than the occasional quick glance at the other woman. When Ally caught one of these looks and smiled Fiona went red and stared intently at the table top.

Montana Smith joined them and sat across from Jiggles, who was far from demure in the looks she lavished on him. "So, Doctor Smith, do you have any exciting tales from this dig?" she asked as the first course was being served.

"Please, call me Montana. Only other academics need to use my title."

"Just Montana? You don't like Monty?"

Montana grimaced, "My father calls me Monty. I prefer the longer version."

"Terribly sorry. Montana it is."

"To answer your question, there haven't been any adventures- really big adventures, anyway- on this excavation. Not yet."

"Doctor Smith's reputation within the archaeology community is most impressive." Amid chipped in, "Many of the students here signed up to experience intrigue and adventure."

"Is that why you're here?" Ginge asked, adjusting his hat as he addressed the younger archaeologist.

"I admit the lure of adventure is strong. But I am really here to find out about my family history. I would greatly like to discover whether my grandmother's takes of our regal lineage are true. When I do that perhaps I shall have tales as tall as Doctor Smith's to tell."

"Not a word of any of the stories I have told you has been a lie. Every one of those things happened." Montana feigned offence at the suggestion that he might embroider, even slightly, when recounting his exploits.

Montana regaled them with tales of pygmy tribes in South America who ate from the skulls of their vanquished foes. He tried to explain how a Roman legionary in full battle gear came to be buried on a remote island in the Atlantic and waxed lyrical about finding treasures on the Silk Road. Then, just as dessert had been served he sighed and said, "But my personal favourite, as far as the reward goes, was the time I tangled with what was known as the Harem of Death. Those ladies sure were.... grateful to be freed. Very grateful."

Fiona's spoon rattled against her dish and bounced across the table as she dropped it. "Oh. Er. Oh." She made a grab for the spoon and only managed to knock over her dessert, spilling it and sauce across the table. "Oh dear." A member of the serving staff was at her shoulder almost immediately, offering a towel.

"Perhaps that story can wait for another day."

Fiona fought her embarrassment and stayed at the table, eagerly tucking in to her replacement pudding to avoid having to say anything.

When they had all finished and were nursing dark, bitter coffees, Montana announced, "Well, we should probably call it a night. Big day tomorrow." He knocked back his coffee and made to stand.

"Would you mind awfully if we went over tomorrow's route before I turn in?" Jiggles asked, "It will save us time in the morning."

"I'll get the charts and meet you at my tent. See you there." With a smile Montana strolled off, tipping his hat onto his head at a jaunty angle. Ally and Ginge both cast Jiggles a knowing look. She gave them a grin. They were getting some- or trying to- so why shouldn't she?

"I guess it is time to turn in." Ginge announced. At least he had the decency not to fake a yawn.

* * *

As soon as he and Amid got back to the tent Ginge started tying up the tent flap. He was as fast as his nimble fingers could manage, but by the time he turned around Amid was already naked. The young Egyptian archaeologist stood on the mat in the middle of the tent and beckoned eagerly. "Come now. I want to see your freckled beast again."

Years of practice saw Ginge bereft of garments almost as fast as Amid and they stood across from each other, admiring the other's body. "I would very much like to take that." Amid pointed at the near erect little Ginge. "In my rear." he added, as if the clarity was needed.

"My pleasure. Do you have any sort of lubricant?"

Amid walked to the wash stand and found a brass vessel. It was spherical, sitting on three short legs. An S-shaped spout came out of the bottom and a wider funnel with a plunger in it rose from the top. The ends of the spout and funnel were linked by thick copper wire which extended into an ornately scrolling handle. Amid motioned for Ginge to hold out his hand whilst he pumped the plunger. A large drop of dark golden oil oozed out of the spout onto Ginge's extended fingers.

"This is very good. A mixture of oils. It is soothing and very very slippery." Amid said with a smile.

Ginge rubbed his fingers together and they slid over each other with almost no resistance. Ginge appreciated the benefits of good lubrication and he nodded approval at how effective this was. Amid smiled at him then pulled a low, wide stool into the middle of the tent. He knelt before it, resting his forearms on the cushioned top.

Amid's buttocks, like the rest of him, were finely formed. They were muscular and tight and his skin was soft and smooth. Ginge took up position behind him and ran fingers over them. He spread them to reveal the puckered hole of Amid's arse, which awaited his attentions.

Ginge started by pumping some of the oil into his left hand then reaching around to cover Amid's impressive erection with it. Thus lubricated it would be ready for his attention later. Next he dribbled some of the oil into the crack between Amid's buttocks. Amid tilted his hips and it pooled around his anus. Now Ginge liberally coated the fingers of his right hand with the oil. He presented his middle finger to Amid's arsehole and swirled it around until every surface was lubricated, then he pushed it in slowly and carefully.

Amid moved against Ginge's questing finger. Encouraged by this reaction, Ginge pushed it in as far as it would go then started moving it in and out as fast as he could. After nearly a minute of this, which drew appreciative grunts from Amid, he slowed again to squirt yet more oil onto his fingers. Now he presented his forefinger too, and it slipped in with ease.

Ginge explored Amid's back passage with his finger tips. The young archaeologist relaxed and took them easily, until Ginge knew he was ready. Clumsily, with two fingers still inside Amid's arse, Ginge pumped oil onto his now rock hard erection. He took little Ginge in his right hand and presented it to Amid's arse just as he pulled his fingers out.

"Oh yes, the freckled monster." Amid sighed as little Ginge pushed past his sphincter. Ginge kept pushing in, further and further, gliding on the oil. Eventually he was completely inside Amid, their balls swinging against each other as they gently rocked. They both groaned with pleasure. Ginge reached under Amid and grasped his stiff penis, running his hand up and down the lubricated shaft.

Ginge started making short thrusts in and out of Amid, matching them with the movements of his hand on the hard cock it held. Amid moved under him, making the thrusts more pronounced. As they sped up Ginge couldn't keep hold of Amid's hard on any longer, but it was twitching with growing excitement all by itself.

With slippery hands making it trickier, Ginge endeavoured to hold on to Amid's waist as his thrusts became ever harder and faster. Amid buried his head in his arms and grunted each time Ginge filled him. His hard cock swung under him, occasionally slapping against his belly and tingling with a building orgasm.

Amid started talking under his breath. Ginge couldn't make out what he was saying, and suspected he would not understand it if he could. Even as he dismissed the incantation, Ginge couldn't shake the feeling that it was affecting him somehow. It was as if the canvas walls of the tent frayed away to reveal the valley as it once was- lush and fertile. The image was complete, with locals and camels looking on appreciatively as he slammed harder and harder into Amid. As he looked around he could see, imagine or hallucinate- whichever best described the vision- other groups crowded around people making love. There were men and men, men and women and women with women, as well as a few groups of three or four tangled together.

Ginge felt a familiar tingling in his hard shaft. His orgasm was very close. The old image of the valley faded away and he was back in the tent pushing hard and deep into Amid. Amid came, spurting thick white semen onto the stool and floor. The muscles of his back passage pulsed in time with his ejaculation, milking Ginge and bringing on his orgasm. The tingle became a warm pulse, sending cum out of his shaft and sparks of electric pleasure up his spine. They cried out in unison as they came together.

* * *

All the way back from the dining tent Fiona walked alongside Ally, but over an arms length to the side. Occasionally she appeared about to say something, only to stop herself and draw slightly further away for a while. Only when they were in their tent could Fiona bring herself to pose her question, "Will Miss Jig.... Er, Jiggles, be returning this evening?"

"Not if she's lucky."

"Oh. Oh.... Do you think she and the Doctor may, er...." Fiona grasped the front of her baggy dress to keep from waving her hands around in any gestures which might reveal how little she understood of the conjugal act. Then she reached her right hand up to her left breast, unconsciously nipping her fingers together to tweak the nipple through several layers of fabric. "But earlier she joined in when you.... I thought she was interested in women, like you are."

"She is, but she's also interested in men. The three of us- Jiggles, Ginge and I- are all interested in both men and women. On balance Jiggles and Ginge are more interested in the chaps whilst I prefer the ladies."

"So it's not.... Unnatural. To feel that way?"

"Not at all." Ally took a step forward and reached out a hand. Fiona didn't step back, but she did release her breast and put her hand out. She grasped Ally's offered hand, but also stopped her coming any closer. Fiona slid her thumb over the palm of Ally's hand, sending tingles up the arm, then gave one of her little smiles before looking down at the ground. "It is time for bed." she announced, "We have a busy day ahead tomorrow."

Ally hid her disappointment the best she could as Fiona went into her bedroom and fastened the hanging door. It had become dark as they talked- night fell quickly in the desert- and Fiona lit the lamp in her room. When she moved it so that she was between the light source and the wall her room shared with Ally's it quickly became obvious that she had learnt from the shadow show earlier. Ally grinned and headed into her own room.

Ally was wearing soft leather desert boots, pale lightweight trousers and a blouse which was fitted close enough to be scandalous. Underneath she had on more utilitarian versions of her usual skimpies- high cut French knickers and a brassiere which squashed her firm round breasts together. She was out of all these clothes in a trice. She moved her bed across until it touched Fiona's through the canvas and stretched out on the cool cotton sheets.

Fiona had been standing, arms clamped over her breasts, whilst she could hear Ally's preparations. Now that her audience was ready she began her show. She reached behind herself and started unfastening her dress. When it was all undone she shrugged her shoulders and let it slide to the floor.

Uncovered Fiona, even as just a silhouette, was far more alluring than the frumpily dressed version, and she was beginning to understand it. She released her under things and put them aside. Naked, she stretched, thrusting her conical breasts out and up, and did a pirouette. Presenting her stunning profile to Ally she reached her right hand up to her left breast again. This time, without fabric restricting her, she squeezed the nipple so hard she surprised herself and emitted a little squeak. On the other side of the canvas Ally mimicked Fiona's move, though she sighed at the exquisite pain she had been expecting. Fiona began running the fingers of both hands over her breasts, paying particular attention to the nipples as they stiffened and extended the cones of gorgeous soft flesh into sharper points.

Unable to stay standing any more, Fiona dropped onto her camp bed, mere inches from Ally who traced the outline of her breast where the shadow was cast onto the canvas. With that piece of whimsy over with Ally got down to the serious business of mirroring Fiona's moves. As they both moved stroking fingers from their breasts down and around their navels their breathing synchronised. From alternating pants and squeals it became stereo moans. Fiona's fingers moved further south, over the slight roundness of her belly and down between her legs. For all her outward innocence it was obvious she had done this before as her index finger bent to explore the slick lips below her pubic hair.

As they both became more excited their thighs lifted and moved apart until their knees touched through the canvas wall. The warmth of the touch was enough to set them off into little exhortations of joy.

"Yes!"

Ally felt the faintest hint of a breeze on her skin. When she opened her eyes she saw star spattered sky above her.

"Yes!"

It was as if the tent was no longer there and Ally and Fiona were pleasuring themselves in the midst of an old Bedouin camp.

"Yes!"

Shadowy figures watched them whilst others made love nearby. It was all so very real, but in the manner of a vivid dream.

"Yes!" "Yes!"

The ghostly watchers didn't bother Ally over much- she had always been something of an exhibitionist. If Fiona even saw them she didn't show any signs of caring.

"Yes! Yes!"

"YesYes!!"

"YeYess!!"

"Yeess!"

"YEEEEEESSS!!!"

The last cry was delivered as a combined scream, at two slightly different pitches, as the girls came together whilst kept apart by a thin wall of fabric. They both sank back into heavy breathing happiness punctuated by joyous shivering after shocks.

Ally held her hand up to the canvas wall and Fiona placed hers against it. "That was incredible." she admitted.

"It was, wasn't it."

"Yes. I've never.... Done that with someone else so near. It was almost as if you were the one doing it to me."

"Would you like that?"

"Well..."

"Maybe tomorrow."

"Maybe. Good night Ally."

"Good night Fiona."

* * *

Jiggles stood outside Montana's tent, wondering how to announce her arrival. "Knock, knock." she said presently.

The flap of the tent opened and Montana stuck his head out. "Isn't that a joke?" he asked.

"I never can remember the punch line. May I come in?"

"You may." Montana pulled the flap wide and presented his tent to her. It was as large as the one the girls shared, but appeared even more spacious as there was no separation of the sleeping and entertaining areas. A travelling bureau was overflowing with papers and artefacts. Maps had been rolled out onto the table beside it, with pieces of ancient stonework at each corner to keep it from curling back up. Jiggles stood over it and studied it. After a few moments she had taken in all of the salient details and pinpointed a number of landmarks she could use for eyeball navigation. "This is the camp, half way up the Valley of the Wizards, and you and old Quince want me to do an aerial survey up this way, towards the head of the valley?"

"That is about it." Montana nodded, "But I have some ideas I have yet to run past the Professor."

"And what would they be?" They were both leaning over the map now, pressing against each other whenever the chance arose.

"I believe there may be a second Valley of the Wizards, an older one. And possibly a third, which would be much more modern. There may still be adherents to the old faith in the hills. That would be interesting." Montana traced a finger from the head of the valley up into the jagged triangles which depicted the hills. "If you go far enough back you come to this lake. Rising out of the lake is this, the new course of the river which used to run through this valley. I believe the old water course has been redirected at, or near, the lake. The map isn't detailed enough to show us where, but water ran down here once." Montana indicated a route from the lake down to the head of the valley. "There's no evidence of the river making it to the sea, or another water course, after it left the Valley of the Wizards. Perhaps it disappeared into the desert eventually, maybe bubbling up at the occasional oasis."

Jiggles leaned over the map to study the areas Montana indicated. "Why would the river change course so drastically?"

"Civil engineering. If you start far enough upstream you can change the course of a river with a few interventions. I've talked to guys from the corps of Engineers about it and they said it was plausible. As well as looking further up the valley for other ruins I'd like to head into the hills and have a look at the area around the lake."

"What would you be looking for?"

"Earthworks, or any other evidence of man-made changes to the river's course. And, to be honest, anything that might add some detail to these maps."

Jiggles laid her hand on top of Montana's. "That sounds like fun."

"Miss Jiggleswick, archaeology is a serious business. It is never fun." Montana opined with a smirk.

"Not even when it leads to the Harem of Death?" Jiggles enquired.

"Well, that was a special case."

"Did any of those oh so grateful ladies teach you any special tricks?"

"One or two."

"Such as?"

"It would be so much easier to show you than to try to explain them." Montana said, raising his eyebrows suggestively.

"Okay." responded Jiggles. She walked to the middle of the room, taking a ribbon from her blouse pocket and using it to tie her hair back. "Please do show me, I'm eager to learn."

For a moment Montana appeared taken aback. This was not how he expected well bred English ladies to behave. On the other hand, it was exactly how he wanted them to behave. Unbuttoning his shirt he approached Jiggles. His chest was honed and muscled, with a light tan and blonde hair. A darker triangle of tanned skin, where his shirt was habitually left open as he worked, pointed down to his crotch. Jiggles was watching him, a warm feeling spreading through her as she grew excited. She was supposed to be playing it cool, but those toned abdominals made it tricky.

Montana reached Jiggles and immediately started unbuttoning her blouse. His fingers were nimble, for all their hard worked roughness, and each little mother of pearl disc popped quickly through the corresponding hole. Jiggles let him get on with it, neither helping nor hindering his efforts. She wasn't exactly passive, however, pushing her chest out when he had removed her blouse, urging him to run his hands over the silky material of her brassiere. Montana duly obliged, squeezing her flesh through the fabric. He found the buttons which held the cups together at the front and released them.

Jiggles' breasts were magnificent, if she admitted so herself. They were full and firm, drooping only slightly once released, and tilting up gently so that her nipples pointed at the far corner of the roof. Montana appreciated them, with eyes and hands, teasing the nipples up to points then squeezing them so that she sighed with pleasure. It was becoming ever harder for her to feign aloofness, her hips were beginning to gyrate. Montana was becoming ever harder as well, she noted with a subtle glance down.

Montana ran his fingers down Jiggles' ribcage to where her trousers rested on her hips. They were darker versions of the loose fitting ones Ally wore- part of a great deal she had done through her family's connections. They were held up by a ribbon belt that was tied at the front. When the bow was released, they would drop straight to the floor. Montana obviously recognised this. He dropped to his knees before her, took the ends between his fingers and tugged at them gently. They both watched the loops of the bow as they decreased and eventually pulled through each other. Jiggles drew a breath and held it.

As a light quiver began in Jiggles' thighs Montana held the ends of the ribbon. He pulled it a little tighter, just to tease, then slowly began releasing the tension. The quiver grew stronger as the material loosened and began sliding down the curve of her hips. Eventually the point of no return was passed and the trousers just dropped to the floor, furling up around Jiggles' feet.

Montana was now face to crotch with Jiggles, with only the peach coloured silk of a pair of provocatively cut knickers between him and her warm pussy lips. He kissed them through the sheer material and she pressed them toward him to increase the contact. There was no point in pretending she wasn't turned on, so she reached down and held Montana's head against her body. His tongue explored her lips through the silk, so intimately the knickers might as well not have been there. When he moved his head back the material was so damp it was practically transparent and he could see the prize.

Pulling Jiggles' knickers down, Montana could smell the musky excitement of her pussy. He savoured it, putting his nose so close that it rustled through her pubic hair. She suppressed a giggle and played her fingers through his hair. His tongue flicked out again, and this time it wet her skin directly. A teasing twirl at the end of the lick drew a long "Ooooohhh." from Jiggles.

Montana sat back and appreciated the view. A finger sneaked up the inside of Jiggles' thigh and slid into her warm wet vagina and she moved against it. Clumsily, she stepped out of her knickers and pants with one foot then kicked them across the tent with the other. She still wore her high ankled desert boots but was otherwise naked. Montana removed his fingers and had her turn around. She thought he wanted her to do a turn so he could take her all in, but he stopped her when she faced away from him, a hand on each of her round buttocks.

Jiggles could feel Montana's breath on the small of her back, so she knew he was leaning in close to her. Then she felt him kiss the triangle of sensitive skin at the top of the cleft between her buttocks. This must be one of the many things the ladies of the harem had taught him. He began kissing each buttock in turn, occasionally sneaking a peck between them. When his tongue teased at the sensitive pucker of her arsehole she shivered, unexpectedly aroused. This was something she hadn't done before. Ginge was all about the bottom play- with other men- and Ally and Jiggles had spent an interesting afternoon one time teasing their fingers into each others' bums, but she had never had her behind excited so by a man. The sheer naughtiness of it turned her on intensely, and she was wet with the excitement. Montana slid a finger into her slick pussy and she moaned.

Jiggles wanted Montana to slide his finger into her bottom, so she could know what it felt like. But she didn't want him to stop moving it in her pussy, particularly when a second joined it. As her excitement mounted he guided her to a pile of cushions and eased her into lying on them on her stomach. She wanted him inside her right now, but he paused to unfasten her boots and remove them, then step back and undress himself. Whilst she waited, Jiggles reached down and slid three of her own fingers into her wet pussy. She looked up at Montana where he stood over her and asked, "Can you fuck me where you were just licking?"

Montana grinned, "Of course. Just a moment." He strode across the tent and picked up a copper jug with an S shaped spout- just like the one Ginge was getting acquainted with at about the same time. He knelt behind her and squirted some of the oil onto his fingers.

"What are you doing?" Jiggles eagerly enquired.

"Wait and see."

Jiggles felt fingers spread the cheeks of her buttocks, exposing her puckered arsehole to Montana's gaze. She started frigging herself harder and faster in response to the thrill. Something, a finger she guessed, pressed against the ring of muscle. She pushed back at it, helping it to ease into her, then sank back down to the cushions as it slid further into her.

Montana moved his finger in and out of Jiggles' behind before removing it to pump out more oil and lubricate things more. The second time he stopped for more oil he eased another finger in beside the first. Jiggles' excitement rose under the ministrations of Montana's and her own fingers, a gyration starting in her hips which gradually sped up until she was practically vibrating. She came with a cry which set the walls of the tent fluttering. As she shook and panted her way down from the plateau Montana removed his fingers. After a liberal application of yet more oil he offered something new to her bottom.

Jiggles realised that Montana's hard penis was nudging at her sphincter. It was bigger, thicker, than his fingers, large enough that it didn't just slide in. Jiggles grasped a cushion with her free hand and tried to hold still despite the shivers which still rippled through her. Montana pushed slowly and gently into her, easing in until, with an almost audible pop, the head of his magnificent erection was past the ring of muscle. He paused there, resting, only to find Jiggle climaxing beneath him. He had to follow her shakes and shimmies just to keep himself lodged in her. As she calmed he started pushing further into her, eliciting more orgasms.

After several ecstatic moments Montana was deep in Jiggles. They were both drenched in sweat and needing a rest. Jiggles' fingers were still moving in her pussy, keeping her warm and instilling little shivers of ongoing joy. With some reluctance she removed the digits and brought the hand up to grasp the pillows and further brace herself. Then she started rotating her hips, pushing them up and down and side to side, moving Montana inside her.

Montana got the message and responded in kind. Short slow thrusts became long slow ones and then faster and faster. Jiggles shook with more orgasms, until she was riding a wave of them, waiting for Montana to come too. The thrusts became shorter again, he grasped her waist tighter and he started making grunting gasps.

Montana stopped, buried as deeply in Jiggles as he could get, and came. Jiggles felt warm spunk filling her insides and it tipped her over into one last mighty orgasm.

* * *

Much later, when Jiggles could walk again and had dressed, she asked Montana, "Did the ladies of the harem teach you any other tricks you can show me?"

"Plenty. Maybe tomorrow I can show you a few of them." Montana was sprawled naked on the cushions. His penis, soft but still engorged and fat, was draped across his thigh. If decorum hadn't decreed that she should be in her assigned tent come dawn she would stay and ravish him some more.

"Oh I do hope so."

Jiggles poked her head out of the tent into the darkness and looked around. But for one fire down by the workings the site was devoid of activity. As her eyes became accustomed to the dark she made out the path she should follow and slipped out of the tent with a rustle of canvas.

The desert was silent. Even in the quiet part of Surrey where Jiggleswick Air had its own landing strip and hangar the night would still hold the rustling sounds of wind through the trees. Here there was nothing save the soft crunch of Jiggles' shoes on the path. So when there was a clatter over to her left she spun towards it, then crouched and froze defensively.

Was it a lion? She wondered. Did they even have lions in this part of North Africa? From the dark she resolved the shape of the supply tents, with the Hooligan and the landing strip beyond them. But there were no more sounds. Probably some scavenging creature had knocked something over trying to get at the food tent and then scarpered.

Jiggles let her heart beat slow some, then stood up straight and looked around, somewhat embarrassed at being so easily spooked. She stared up at the familiar constellations, sharp in the clear desert sky, as if she needed them to navigate her way back to the tent.

Back at the tent it was obvious that the occupants were in their own rooms and had failed to double up as Ally had so obviously desired. It would be impolite to stink so much of sex in the morning, so Jiggles stripped and endeavoured to wash herself the best she could from the basin. Jiggles admired her own breasts before soaping them up and gently cleaning them. As she teased suds onto her stiff but tender nipples she glanced in the mirror again and spotted, over her shoulder, that the flap to Fiona's bedroom had been pushed slightly open. She paused at the sight, just long enough for Fiona to realise she had been rumbled and close the flap.

Jiggles cursed her reaction, silently and with a wry smile, and went back to her ablutions. When she next gave the mirror a passing glance she spotted that the flap had teased open again.

Fiona knew her peeping had been observed, but she carried on regardless. Jiggles knew she was being watched but resolved not to play to the audience too much. It was the unspoken pact of voyeur and willing exhibitionist.

Jiggles turned to face Fiona's tent, but twisted her upper body and head to try to see her own behind in the mirror. As she soaped the half moons of her buttocks she pretended to unconsciously present the puffy engorged lips of her labia to Fiona's gaze.

The only thing that surprised Jiggles was that she didn't hear the muted sighs and quiet slaps of someone trying to masturbate silently. Perhaps Fiona was saving up the sight for later.

Being watched kept Jiggles' excitement levels high. But she was really too tired to do anything about it. She flashed Fiona her most private parts- and hoped the girl enjoyed it- as she washed, and savoured the warmth it kept in her. But when she was clean she simply climbed into her bed and went straight to sleep.

* * *

Morning broke with the same speed as night had fallen. There was some warning, to those who had woken in time, as the sky turned copper then gold, before the sun broke cover and bright warm rays cut through the canvas. Jiggles, who had been dog tired after her late night escapades, surprised herself with the speed at which she transitioned from asleep to fully awake.

Ally was up and about almost as quickly, and Fiona poked her head out at the sounds of water in the basin.

They stood naked around the wash stand, Jiggles and Ally either side of Fiona and feigning accidental brushes against her skin. She didn't flinch at the contact. Indeed, she appeared to be glowing, rather than blushing, because of it. More than once she turned slightly towards Jiggles, as if about to ask a question, before thinking better of it. Ally rested a hand on the girl's back and asked for her. "Fiona and I would love to know how your meeting with the dashing Doctor Smith went last night." Fiona thought of protesting, but decided that yes, she would like to know about it actually, and kept silent.

"It was incredible." Jiggles sighed. "Those harem ladies were very good teachers. He passed on some new tricks to me." Before she could expand upon her comment the breakfast horn sounded. "I suppose we should get dressed. Perhaps I can tell you more about it later."

"Perhaps I can learn some new tricks myself." Fiona said with a sideways glance at Ally.

* * *

Fiona wore a practical one piece get up, somewhere between dungarees and one of Ginge's pairs of overalls, with a blouse underneath to cover her arms and shoulders. A floppy brimmed hat kept the sun off her pale skin. The outfit was a pleasing change from the sack she had worn the day before. If anything it was cut a little small, so that the material stretched taut over her shapely buttocks when she bent over. Ally noted the buttons atop the shoulder straps and down the side as far as her hips, just in case she needed to release them in a hurry later.

They met Ginge at the food tent, where he was talking with Amid and another man. The man nodded and walked off after a last few words with Amid. "Will you need me on your little jaunt today?" Ginge asked Jiggles.

"I shouldn't think so. It is only a little local flight after all."

"That is useful." Amid said, "As it appears we are in need of Ginge's mechanical expertise. Both the supply truck and Model T runabout are not working this morning. We need to send the truck for supplies today as we are near the limit of our stocks."

"Both vehicles broke down at the same time?" Ally pondered aloud.

Amid's face clouded, as though he were considering sinister implications. "Yes. It is imperative that at least one of them be made operational this morning."

"Well Ginge is your mechanic for that." Ally reassured. "Come to think of it, do you need a co-pilot today?" she asked, "I might stay here and find out more about Fiona.... And her job here at the dig." There was an unspoken nod that this would allow both Jiggles and Ally extra time alone with the current objects of their lust.

"Oh I should cope well enough. The Doctor seems quite a capable chap should there be any problems."

As if conjured up by mention of his name, Montana appeared. "Are we ready for today's reconnaissance?" he asked as they sat down. After a brief explanation of the rota change he cast knowing glances at Amid and Ginge and Ally and Fiona then shared a grin with Jiggles.

After breakfast they all walked out to the airstrip. Ginge, Ally and Jiggles prepped the aeroplane whilst Fiona helped Montana and Amid load camera equipment aboard. In short order they were ready and Jiggles fired up the engines. As the props got up to speed Ginge, Amid, Ally and Fiona scuttled away from the dust and sand they raised.

The Hooligan bumped over to the start of the runway then Jiggles throttled up and it accelerated away. For a worrying moment the plane was raising so much dust that it disappeared from sight. Then it appeared from the top edge of the beige billows and climbed rapidly away.

* * *

Jiggles did a circuit of the dig site, waggling the wings as the Hooligan crossed the airstrip. After they had shaken and slapped a large amount of desert off their clothing and out of their hair the ground crew turned back to the camp. The vehicles were parked nearby, Ginge started sauntering toward them. As they were practically on the path back to the dig the others followed him. "What do you have by way of tools?" he asked Amid

"There is a toolbox in the truck, but I am not an expert so I do not know how good it is."

"Ginge is the master of making do with what's at hand." Ally reassured, "He only needs things that look vaguely like tools and he can usually get the job done."

When they reached the battered old Fordson, Ginge clambered aboard and found the metal box bolted to the bed behind the cab. He studied the contents, shaking his head theatrically, before pronouncing, "That'll do." He started laying the tools out on the wood of the bed, sorting them by type.

"We should get to the dig." Fiona announced.

"I shall stay here with Ginge. If there is something suspicious about these break downs I would like to know as soon as possible." Amid declared. As Fiona and Ally walked off he climbed up into the truck bed and stood behind Ginge.

* * *

Quince was fussing around the site, telling the highly skilled local workers how to do their jobs as if they were children. Eustace followed behind, making notes and occasionally brushing away dust with a look of disgust. "Ah, Fiona, where have you been?" Without showing that an answer was expected, Quince waddled over to the nearest table and picked up several pieces of pottery. Before the bemused gaze of the man who had been working on them and sorting out other matching shards, he pieced them together like an ancient jigsaw. "There, like that. It is really awfully simple you know." He turned back to Fiona, Ally and Eustace. "Really. I thought that Smith had a reputation for getting things done quickly. Perhaps too quickly. Not so slow, anyway. Where the deuce is Smith? Does anyone know?"

"He just took off with Miss Jiggleswick to take aerial photographs of the valley." Fiona informed him.

"He did? Well that's a bit.... Oh, now wait, that was my idea wasn't it. Very good, very good. Fiona my dear, are you ready to sketch the hieroglyphs before we take the stone off this tomb?"

"Yes I am, professor." Fiona patted her shoulder bag.

"Good show. Well come along then, they should have uncovered it by now."

* * *

Ginge had tried a couple of times to get the truck to start before giving a grim nod. When he had undone the fuel line he squeezed some of the liquid from it onto his fingers and sniffed them. He nodded again, "Water." he told Amid.

"Really?"

"And perhaps a bit of sand, just to make cleaning the lines trickier."

"So it is sabotage?"

"Yes. Well, mischief might be a better description. This can be fixed in a few hours. It may hold you up, but it isn't going to stop the dig."

"Unless they only want to keep the vehicles here for a short while. Long enough to carry out some other plan." After voicing these somewhat cryptic worries Amid clambered onto the roof of the truck cab and stared down the wide valley. Spotting something which caused him worry he shouted to a pair of local workers who were checking the packing of artefacts in their crates. He dropped from the cab to the soft sand and waited for them.

When the two workers arrived Amid had a rapid conversation with them, pointing down the valley then up it before taking the tallest man's hand in an odd grasp and shaking it. The two men hurried off, the shorter one into the camp, the taller toward the camel enclosure.

"Trouble?" Ginge simply asked when Amid returned.

"Quite possibly. Someone is coming this way. In motor vehicles judging by the dust cloud. I do not doubt that their motives are bad." Amid set off for the body of the dig and the command tent.

"Bandits?" Ginge asked, jumping down to follow Amid.

"Grave robbers," Amid nodded, "possibly. Though disabling the vehicles is more sophisticated than they usually are."

"If they scuppered the vehicles why didn't they...." They both stared at the sky up the valley, where the Hooligan wasn't even a speck, then started running for the radio tent.

✳ ✳ ✳

The large stone, which capped who knew what, had been cleared of sand. The whole hieroglyph message had been revealed, along with the edges where the stone butted up against other pieces of hewn rock. Fiona considered the rock before walking around the hole to find the best view. "I think it is warning us not to lift it." she told Ally as she pulled out her pad of paper.

"Like a 'No Trespassing' sign?"

"Maybe. Normally they would name the deity who would strike you down, but I can't see any god symbols that I recognise. It may be some sort of safety warning, telling us it is dangerous to enter."

Ally studied the carvings. "You get all of that from this?" Fiona nodded. Ally looked again. "Is that a duck?"

Fiona glanced over the top of her pad. "Probably not. It's all just a foreign language, like any other, albeit not used by anyone still alive." She was making quick marks on the paper. When she had a basic drawing of the warning she took the paper she had scribed it on, folded it and put it into the front pocket of her outfit. "I like to keep a copy for myself, so I can examine it later. And it helps me remember the orientation of all the symbols when I'm putting together the big final image."

"Why not just take a photograph?"

"Oh there will be photographs, later, but they still can't capture all the details the way my pencil and paper can. This will be quite boring I'm afraid. I become quite engrossed in my work."

"Oh, that is alright. If I get bored I shall go and have a look in the other holes."

Ally watched Fiona sketch for a while. She had an intense expression of concentration and whilst Ally wanted to ask questions she knew better than to break the spell. Enchanting as it was, after a while she felt the need to have a look around.

As she climbed out of the hole, Ally noticed that there weren't as many workers around as there had been the previous day. She wasn't familiar with how archaeological digs worked, perhaps fewer chaps were needed the further back through history you went. Then she noticed that few of the other holes had crews around them either.

This seemed a curious turn. Ally climbed a spoil heap and looked around. There was activity, but it wasn't anywhere on the site. Down the valley, to the North of the camp, a crowd had gathered on the road. Beyond them dust rose from traffic coming along the road. Under the cloud she could just about make out the square shape of a vehicle, and at least one more beyond it.

As Ally squinted she heard angry voices either side of the spoil heap. She looked down to see a gang of workers running toward the crowd. Several of them carried rifles, of various vintages. One of them, spotting the bemused woman atop the rubble, stopped to shout out, "Bandits! Grave robbers! They come to steal treasures and take foreigners! You must run!" Then he was gone before Ally could request more details.

There was a crackling from down the valley. When Ally looked she could see tiny puffs of smoke rising from the crowd where ancient black powder guns had been fired. The object that had been raising the dust cloud split and became five vehicles which fanned out and bounced across the desert.

Being a charter pilot opened up opportunities for plenty of adventure and occasional danger. Ally recognised that this was one of those occasions. She started scurrying down the spoil heap. The surface was loose under foot and she slid a short way with each step, so she adjusted her gait to compensate. She tripped and stumbled at the base of the pile, but was quickly back on her feet.

Fiona didn't look up until Ally clattered down the ladder nearest her. She glanced around the empty hole, confused, before Ally grabbed her arm.

"We need to go!" Ally tugged at Fiona's arm.

"What's happening?"

"We're being attacked!"

"Oh my." Fiona had her pad in her bag and the bag on her shoulder in one fluid move. She looked down at the pencils and brushes she had scattered, but quickly decided against gathering them up. "Which way?" she asked.

"I don't know. Out of the hole first."

They were half way up the first ladder when there was an explosion near the top edge of the hole. It threw the ladder backwards, tossing them off, then showered dust, sand and stone down on them.

* * *

The radio tent was a small adjunct to the office tent, identifiable by the tall whip antenna attached to one corner. It was dark after the bright sunlight, and they stood blinking for a few moments to adjust to the gloom. As soon as they did it became obvious that something was amiss.

The radio set had been pulled forward on the table and was slightly askew. As Ginge turned it around he could see that the back panel had been prised off. Valves had been pulled from their mountings and wires had been cut. Ginge wasn't as adept with electrics as with mechanical bits. If he could find the components he might be able to make the radio work again, but it would take at least a day longer to fix than he had available.

"The workers will mount a resistance, but we should get out of the camp until we know it is safe." Amid declared, "I shall go and find Quince and Eustace, you should get Fiona and Ally."

Ginge nodded agreement. He swept the radio tent's flap aside, and they almost immediately found the Professor and his assistant.

Quince was standing near the corner of the office tent, facing away from them. He had his hands raised, because Eustace was behind him, pressing a small, but nonetheless deadly, gun into his back. They were both staring North, toward the crowd ready to repel their attackers, but started to turn at the noise from the radio tent.

Amid grabbed Ginge and pulled him back into the tent. He drew a short blade from a hidden scabbard and slashed an opening in the rear wall which they rushed out of as Eustace started firing.

Eustace fired three unaimed shots into the tent- doing little more than put some holes into the fabric- before turning back to Quince. The Professor was thinking about running, but a whack about the back of the head dropped him to the ground. Eustace strode to the tent, gun at the ready, walked through and stepped out of the impromptu exit. Amid and Ginge had disappeared.

* * *

Ally's world was moving around her in twists and curves and there was dust in her eyes and mouth. She shook her head and small stones and dust fell from her hair. The ground steadied and she got a look around. Fiona was just a stretch of her arm away, lying on her back and examining her outfit where the straps had broken. They had been thrown all the way back into the bottom of the hole and now lay on top of the hieroglyph covered cap stone. In unison they started struggling up.

When they were both half stood there was another explosion near the top edge of the hole. This one threw debris into the far corner of the hole, though small stones skittered across to where they stood and fine dust billowed over them. Ally looked down, and swept sand aside with her foot. "Was the stone cracked before?" she asked.

Whilst the sounds of battle swirled around the edges of the hole and more dust and stones plumed up from explosions, Ally and Fiona studied the jagged, and quite obviously new, break in the surface they stood on. "That's not good." Fiona asserted, just before the section she stood on shifted and started falling.

Ally made a grab for Fiona, managing to get a handful of material. Fiona's blouse tore as Ally tried to keep her from tumbling into the dark with the section of stone, and her brassiere popped open. Fiona pulled Ally down and she landed hard on the stone, head and shoulders over the edge as she held on to Fiona's clothes.

The buttons on the side of Fiona's one piece suit started popping off. She squealed as each one gave way. Ally felt herself move further over the edge with each jerking drop The stone underneath her was moving as well, slowly tipping up to slide her into the dark. But for some reason all Ally could think of, as the last of the fastenings gave way, was that there were worse final sights than the marvellous breasts before her, which stood out pale and firm against the pitch black below them.

The stone tipped, sliding Ally into the darkness. She tumbled after Fiona, trying to catch her. Neither of them thought to scream.

* * *

Jiggles had perfected the technique of dipping one wing so as to give Montana a better angle for his photographs. They worked their way through the points of interest on the map making passes from the North and then the South. With Quince's targets ticked off they continued on toward Montana's.

The valley narrowed and grew steeper, ending in a cliff wall over a hundred feet tall. Above the cliff face stretched a plateau, a river glinting in the sunlight on the far side. "Is that the river you think ran down the Valley of the Wizards?" Jiggles asked.

"It certainly is. If we head West we should find the source."

Jiggles followed the directions and soon realised they were flying over a long dead river bed. Surely this was where the river which fed the Valley of the Wizards had flowed before tumbling over the cliffs. From the North another dead river converged with the one they were tracking. They never quite intersected. After a while the current course of the river dog-legged in toward them. All three originated from the large lake at the Western end of the plateau.

Montana was checking what he saw below against diagrams in a small leather notebook. "Is it what you were expecting?" Jiggles asked.

"I believe it is." Montana replied with a smile. "How long can we spend taking pictures of it?"

"Oh, a while, the first reserve tank is full. In fact," Jiggles checked gauges, "we should switch over to it now." She reached across and changed the fuel source.

In a matter of moments it became obvious that something was wrong. The motor on the right wing spluttered and lost power. The left engine joined in the off tune clattering.

"What's the problem?" Montana asked as Jiggles switched the fuel supply back.

"Something in the fuel lines. It has to have come from the reserve tank. I'm going to try flushing the pipes. If that doesn't work, we shall have to land."

"Anything I can do?"

Jiggles considered this for a moment before the engines answered for her, both stopping at once. "No." she said, honestly. "Hold on tight and hope we don't end up in the lake."

Without its engines the Hooligan slowed and started dropping from the sky.

Part 2

No light entered the buried room and, but for the rustle of flowing sand, it was utterly silent.

As Ally took stock of her situation she knew she should be scared, but found herself serene and unworried. This was probably because her right hand clasped a fine, firm conical breast and her cheek rested on its sister. The lovely chest rose and fell as its gorgeous owner breathed deeply.

After another happy minute on Fiona's bosom, Ally reluctantly roused herself. She felt around the perky breast she held, moving up it until she was squeezing a stiffening nipple. Fiona sighed and moved under her.

They were tangled together on a deep bed of fine grained sand on a slight incline. As Ally searched around her she found chunks of the stonework which had fallen with them into the pit. They had been lucky not to be crushed or battered by the rocks as they tumbled.

As she stretched her arms and legs to check they still worked, Ally stared up into the darkness. She remembered how they came to be down here in the bowels of the earth. Up above them- how far she did not know- was an archaeological dig in the Valley of the Wizards. Jiggleswick Air had flown Fiona, her boss and his other assistant to this disputed part of North Africa the day before, to help with the dig. After bonding, rather erotically, with Fiona the night before, Ally had been with her in the main pit of the dig, studying hieroglyphs on the capping stone that now lay in pieces around them, when the site was attacked. Explosions had rocked the ground around the hole, cracking the stone and dropping Ally and Fiona into a chamber which hadn't been opened in centuries.

Fiona sighed and stretched. She made a strange little squeak at the sensation of sand rubbing against her smooth skin and brought a hand up to find Ally's and bring it back to her breast. She encouraged Ally's fingers to keep on tweaking the nipple. "Are we dead?" she asked breathlessly.

Ally considered the warm flesh she was appreciating and hazarded a guess, "I don't think so."

"It is so dark. I can't see anything." Fiona's other nipple moved against Ally's cheek as she spoke and she instinctively turned her head to take it between her lips. "It seems I have no clothes on." Fiona announced.

Ally released Fiona's nipple. "They tore off just before we fell down here. Except for your knickers, maybe."

"My knickers?" Fiona pushed Ally's hand off her breast and moved it down her ribcage and tummy. It stopped for a moment at her belly button as she giggled, then carried on down until it reached the fine material of her knickers. "Oh yes, those are still there." She pushed Ally's fingers under the edge of the material and left them there. Ally took the hint and started swirling Fiona's lush pubic bush.

Fiona's free hand had come up to rest on the back of Ally's head, urging her to take in more of the breast. "Maybe." she started, "Maybe we should try to find a way out of here." The thought shuffled out of her mind as Ally's forefinger found her clitoris. She pushed up against the touch, trying to urge the finger into her.

Ally reached lower, hooking her finger around as it slid into Fiona. She pushed another digit in, it was so hot and slippery. Fiona moaned. This was what they had both wanted to do the night before, when they had masturbated together whilst separated by the canvas wall of their tent. Ally just wished that she could see Fiona in her ecstasy.

Fiona was grinding against Ally's fingers, releasing the grip on her head. Ally looked up and around, to see if her eyes had adjusted to the light. Instead, she found she was having the strangest vision. Whilst it was still pitch black and she could not see the beautiful girl who writhed under her ministrations there were still images forming before her eyes.

The woman who ground and moaned as Ally's fingers probed deep inside her was just as gorgeous as Fiona, if in different ways. She had wider hips- giving a more pronounced waist- darker skin and a rounder face. She had big brown eyes which stared unfocussed at the ceiling as she praised Ally's technique in an unknown language. Ally knew she was making love to Fiona, not this ghost, and managed to still her surprise enough that she barely faltered. Fiona still noticed the missed beat in the rhythm of Ally's fingering and asked, "Is something wrong?"

"No, not at all." They searched for each other's lips and kissed. Ally slipped a third finger into Fiona, so slick with excitement was she.

When she came up for air Ally looked around, and saw the chamber as it had once been. Large oil lamps lit the scene as naked attendants bustled around. Animal headed statues stared down at Ally and Fiona, lascivious approval upon their anthropomorphic visages.

There were six walls to the room. The nearest one held a large door, the massive stone uprights and lintel framing heavy wood with brass fittings. As Ally watched, one of the naked attendants put a small lamp in an alcove then pushed the doors apart easily. Behind it was a long corridor lit by more oil lamps. The attendant walked through, the door closed behind her and the spell was broken. Without missing a stroke, Ally continued making love to Fiona.

Fiona's legs had spread wider as Ally's fingers moved in her. Ally clamped her thighs around the nearest of the akimbo limbs and pushed against it. She hadn't realised just how close to orgasm she was herself, and the frottage quickly moved her closer. Fiona's hands clasped over Ally's, urging her to frig harder and faster until they both came together. Their cries echoed around the chamber, hardly dying away before their breathing had calmed down again.

As they cuddled close afterwards Fiona asked, "Are we trapped here?"

"I don't know. Possibly not." Ally struggled to reach into her pocket and draw out a slim elegant cigarette lighter. She hinged the top off and flicked at the wheel which ground sparks from the flint. In the deep blackness of the chamber each little hot dot shone like a star. On the third strike the petrol soaked wick caught and the two women were illuminated. The flame was blinding after the darkness they had made love in, though in reality it produced only a small sphere of yellow light around them. The tops of Fiona's breasts were highlighted by the flickering light whilst the shadows they cast danced around as the flame wavered.

Now there was light some of Fiona's innate shyness surfaced and she covered her breasts as her cheeks reddened. She looked away from Ally for a moment and when she turned back her hand dropped from her bosom again and she smiled nervously. "If we can get out of here can we do that in the light? And without your clothes on? I would like to see you. And have you see me."

"Of course darling." Ally stood and helped Fiona up. The gentle slope of sand they stood on ran down in the direction of the door Ally had seen in her vision, so she started in that direction.

"Hold on a moment." Fiona said, "Could you hold the light over there?"

Ally turned and held the lighter up and Fiona used its meagre light to pull a piece of clothing and a shoulder bag from where they had been partially covered by sand and light rubble. She held up the torn remnants of the one piece work suit she had been wearing before tumbling into the hole. The buttons which fastened up either side had mostly popped off and the openings had torn most of the way to the knees but the shoulder straps looked like they would still fasten. There was no sign of the blouse or brassiere she had been wearing underneath. "I hope you do not mind if I cover up." Fiona apologised as she pulled the dungarees on, "But it might be best."

Ally was a touch disappointed that she was no longer accompanied by a nearly naked woman, but had to accept the practicalities. They were trapped in an ancient underground complex and she couldn't think about sex all the time if they were to get out.

Fiona found that the right shoulder strap would fasten and the top button on the left slit was still in place. From the side, particularly the right, the full swell of a breast could still be seen, but she was significantly more decent overall. She slung her bag, which still contained some art materials not scattered in the fall, over her shoulders and stood up straight. "There. I am almost ready for polite society again." she announced.

"You are beautiful. Polite society doesn't deserve you." Ally told her. "This way."

The lighter was growing warm, and no doubt running low on fuel, but in only a few careful steps they stood before the giant door. Ally searched around the frame and, sure enough, there was the alcove she had seen in her vision. She pulled the lamp out. It looked like a narrowed and stretched teapot made of brass, with a wick protruding from the spout. She put the lighter's dying flame to the damp material and it lit immediately. She flipped the lighter closed and waved it around to try to cool it. In the last couple of seconds it had become too warm to be comfortable.

Fiona had been studying the stone door frame, running her hands over the surface. Now the lamp illuminated the whole opening and she took a step back to stare up and around at it. "Oh my." she managed to say after a moment. "How.... how did you know to find this? You came straight to it."

Ally couldn't bring herself to describe the vision she had seen whilst they were making love. She could hardly bring herself to believe it either. "I have very good night vision." she managed to lie after a moment.

They walked the breadth of the double doors and found another lamp in a matching alcove on the other side of the frame. Before offering it up to be lit Fiona squeezed some oil from the wick and rubbed it between her fingers. "This is odd." she opined.

"How so?"

"Well, over time lamp oil thickens. In a tomb which has been abandoned as long as this one it should be like candle wax, or maybe even harder. This feels almost fresh, as if the lamp were topped up recently."

"Perhaps we have been lucky and it has kept incredibly well."

"Perhaps....." Neither of them voiced the other possible conclusion.

"Shall we try to find a way out?" Ally suggested after a while.

"Do you think this door will open?"

"There is only one way to find out."

They placed the lamps on the floor behind them and each pushed hard against one of the doors. They did not open as easily as they had in Ally's vision, but they did move and there was soon a large enough gap to step through without squeezing.

Before they left the chamber Fiona looked back. In the lamp light all but the farthest corners were visible. The slope of rubble and sand they had ridden into the room took up half of it. There was a shadowed indentation near the bottom of the debris where they had woken and made love. "Should we maybe stay here and wait for someone to dig down to us?" Fiona suggested.

"We could. But what if the people who dig down are the ones who attacked the camp?" Ally replied. "And wouldn't you rather explore- and maybe find your own way out- than feign helplessness and wait for someone else's help?"

Fiona stepped through the doors and held her lamp up. It illuminated a long straight passage, disappearing into darkness. She turned to Ally. "Let's explore."

* * *

Ginge was in the bottom of a trench, under boards which feet were hammering over. His vision was dominated by the soles of the shoes- and occasionally the legs and tight muscular buttocks- of Amid, his lover from the night before. Amid was an Egyptian archaeology student, descended from a long line of tomb robbers and – allegedly- royalty, who worked with the American archaeologist Montana Smith running the dig in the Valley of the Wizards. Ginge suspected the tricks of the family trade had been well learned by his guide.

Mere moments before, they had been in the dig's radio tent. The equipment had been sabotaged so they couldn't contact Jiggles- flying Jiggleswick Air's Hawker Hooligan biplane further up the Valley- or the authorities. Then things had taken a turn for the worse. Stepping out of the tent they had found Professor Horatio Quince- the famed Egyptologist they had flown into the country- with a gun pointed at his back. Holding the gun was the Professor's upper class twit of an assistant, Eustace. Amid had reacted swiftly, slicing a hole in the rear of the tent and dragging Ginge through it before Eustace started shooting at them.

Now they were struggling through this secret gap under the walkway laid in one of the archaeological dig's old trenches as the mysterious attackers ran to and fro overhead. The assault on the dig had all happened so fast that Ginge hadn't had a chance to see any of the raiders. Amid had made a few remarks about their techniques- someone, probably Eustace, had sabotaged the dig's vehicles as well as the radio- which suggested that these were not the usual bandits. There had been a hint of professional and family disdain at the brazenness they exhibited.

Amid abruptly halted and Ginge very nearly shuffled into his feet. To Amid's left there was a section of the wall blocked off with planking, which he started struggling to push to the side. Another narrow tunnel was revealed, and Amid arched and squirmed into it. Ginge closed his eyes and took a breath before following. He had never suffered from claustrophobia, but if he spent much more time down here he might begin to.

The new tunnel was dark, and Ginge just kept on crawling into the black until he bumped into Amid's soles. Amid had stopped to push at something ahead and after a few scrunching grinding noises it gave way. The tunnel lit up as it saw sunshine again and it was so bright Ginge's eyes stung. Amid popped forward to stick his head out of the hole and have a look around, then shot out. Ginge followed, trying to be as nimble.

Ginge tumbled out of the hole and down a bank of sand, stone and spill from the dig. He found himself in the bottom of a dry ravine, surrounded by swirling dust. When he reorientated himself he stared up the slope to see Amid closing up the hole with a square section of wood and hiding it under sand. He motioned Ginge toward him.

When Ginge had scrabbled up the scree Amid finished patting down the dirt and signalled toward the top of the bank. They crawled up slowly and peeked over it. They were far enough from the dig site, and on the side away from the action, that they faced little risk of being seen. However, they were close enough to make out some details.

The raiding party had arrived in motor vehicles- large, military-looking lorries, in fact. Most of them wore a uniform the colour of sand, but they seemed to be taking orders from civilians, including Eustace. The troops had rounded up most of the workers from the dig, including those injured in the assault. A few of the crew were arguing with Eustace and his cronies. After a while Eustace made a dismissive gesture and soldiers herded the workers back to the main group then started moving them toward the road away from the dig.

"Where are they going?" Ginge asked.

"Away." Amid said with a shrug. "The delegation would have argued that they were just workers and should be let free. The raiders, whoever they are, know that most of them tried to defend the site but that they can't just kill them or even keep them."

"So they just get to walk away?"

"It is a long way from here to the nearest town, particularly with the wounded. Some of them may still die on the way."

"That's....."

"Harsh. I know. The desert is a hard place, and my people are hard to cope with it."

"There is a lot you haven't told us isn't there?"

"Indeed there is. Come with me and I shall endeavour to answer some of the questions you no doubt have."

They slid down the bank and Amid led the way along the ravine.

* * *

The water was cool, almost chilling, against her skin, but after the heat and dust Jiggles relished it. Another couple of strokes took her to the bed of the lake. There was no silt on the section below her, and in the crystal clear water she could make out the pattern of ancient tool markings. It appeared that a notch had been cut out of the rock to guide the water flow. She looked around and saw the jumble of stones where the channel had later been blocked.

By now Jiggles' lungs were burning, so she twisted and kicked upwards. As her head and shoulders broke the surface she swished her hair around and scattered shimmering droplets about her. She took a deep breath before dropping back under the water then bobbing gently. Naked, she settled on her back, amused by the way her breasts thrust out of the water and were lapped by tiny waves, then gently paddled her way back to the shore where Montana Smith waited.

As Jiggles rose, Aphrodite-like, from the lake, Montana stood and held out her blouse. Much as he appreciated her voluptuous nudity he was gentleman enough to help her cover herself if she wished. "Thank you Doctor, but I don't think I shall dress just yet. I hope you don't mind."

"Not at all. Not at all." They had laid a heavy blanket on the ground and Montana watched as Jiggles sat on it, leant back on her elbows and stretched and spread her legs. They shared a grin.

"Can you not swim?" Jiggles asked.

"I'm afraid I never learnt. I grew up a long way from the sea and miles from the nearest river or lake. There was never the call for it."

"There is definitely evidence of workings. You think this is the channel that fed the river in our Valley of the Wizards?"

"The beginning of it, at least. There were some structures further down the valley which would have tweaked the flow to get it into our valley."

"When we get the kite back in the air we have a lot of interesting stuff to report to Quince." They both stared at the plane Jiggles had managed to coax to a rough landing a couple of hours earlier. "If we get the kite back in the air."

Jiggleswick Air's Hawker Hooligan had slewed around as it neared the edge of the lake when the left wheel had dug in to a rut. They hadn't been rolling very fast so damage had been minimal. Of course, there was still the question of why the aeroplane's engines had both died. Jiggles suspected sugar or water in the secondary fuel tank, but tracing it could involve going through all the fuel lines. Once the problem was resolved, they still had to get it turned around and moved to a stretch of flat land long enough for take off.

If Ginge had been with them he would already have found the problem with the engines and straightened the wheel. But they had left him behind, thinking they were going on a simple little jaunt up the valley, so he could spend some time with Montana's assistant Amid. Jiggles might have cursed decisions made in the name of sex, but couldn't bring herself to. She could- and would when she got around to it- clean out the fuel lines herself but had chosen to take her clothes off and entice Montana instead.

The night before Jiggles and Montana had made love in his tent and he had introduced her to anal intercourse- something she had dallied in with Ally and a dildo, but never had a chance to try with a man. It was one of the many tricks Montana said he had learnt from the ladies of the Harem of Death, and she wanted to find out what else they had taught him.

The day before, Montana had been all business, dressed in a linen suit and looking just as a western academic in North Africa should. He had also been visibly uncomfortable in the costume. He was far more at ease in the worn and weathered garb he sported today. His wide brimmed hat shaded his face, occasionally throwing it entirely into shadow, and the loose fitting shirt and trousers allowed for easy movement. For the first time Jiggles noticed the bull whip on his belt. "Do you know how to use that?" she asked, pointing at it.

For a moment Montana thought she was referring to his penis. Then he remembered the coil of leather on his hip. He unclipped it and let it unfurl. A couple of twitches sent waves along its length and stretched it out on the ground pointing away from them. "Edna has saved my life on more than a few occasions."

"Edna?"

"After a teacher I once had. Don't you have a name for your plane?"

"We used to call it Bertie. But then we met a test pilot who impressed the three of us, so we renamed it Bendy after him."

"Bendy?"

"He was.... flexible. Sexually. If you get my meaning."

"Ah, right. Like Amid. Or your man Ginge if I'm not mistaken."

"But not you?"

"I won't judge any man or woman for how they get their jollies, so long as they're doing it with other consenting adults. When you study history, particularly the more lurid parts, you find all sorts of combinations were favoured in the past. But when it comes to man lovin' the idea just doesn't excite me." Montana paused. "See that stone?" he pointed.

Jiggles sat up and stared where Montana was pointing. "Yes." she acknowledged.

"Watch." With one sinuous move Montana flicked the length of the whip into the air then swung it toward the stone. Jiggles didn't really see Edna connect with her target, but there was a loud snap and the stone bounced almost straight up then arced away to bounce down to the lake shore. Before she'd even noticed it landing, Jiggles realised that Edna had coiled up on her body. The tasselled tip tickled at her navel and the length trailed up her belly and over her breasts, tickling her nipples into stiffness. "What about you? I sense that you and Miss Ally may well keep each other warm on those cold English nights."

"We certainly do." Jiggles arched her back to make the soft braided leather of Edna rub against her nipples. She ran her hand up the shaft of the whip, grasping it as near to the handle as she could. Montana got the message- Jiggles wished to become better acquainted with Edna. "And we have other ways of entertaining ourselves. Let me show you."

Edna's handle, stiff wood wrapped in braids of soft leather, was ten inches long. A thick pommel marked the base of the handle, to make it easier to hold, and there was a leather wrist strap for added security. The pommel reminded Jiggles of just one thing, and they both knew exactly where it was going. Grasping the handle in both hands she lay back and tickled the top of her thighs with the strap.

Jiggles teased her vagina lips with the strap then ran it up and down the inside of her thighs, slapping them gently with it. She was just about to introduce the pommel to the slick crinkled lips of her vagina when a shadow crossed her face. She opened her eyes and stared up to see Montana standing naked, but for his hat, over her. His fantastic penis bobbed in her line of sight and they grinned at each other. "Would you like to swap places with Edna?" Jiggles asked.

"Let her have her fun. I was just wondering if I could join in.... Elsewhere."

Jiggles grinned and gave a little nod at the space to the left of her head. Montana knelt down quickly and then bent over her to present his deep red glans to her lips. She closed her eyes and purred against the warm flesh. Then she pushed the knob of Edna's handle past her slick lower lips, gasped with pleasure and took a length of Montana into her throat.

The whip slipped and slithered over Jiggles' belly and nipples as she twisted the handle around to feed it further into herself. Montana thrust gently in and out of her mouth, loving the feel of her tongue moving on his hot glans. "Oh, yeah." he moaned. Jiggles echoed him- as best she could around the hard on in her mouth.

Jiggles drew her feet up and angled her hips. She began moving Edna back and forth inside her. The larger head at the end of the thinner shaft felt different to any penis or even dildo she had experienced before, and she always enjoyed new sensations. After a couple of thrusts the strap was inside her as well and it curled and wrapped around the knob to give her different sensations with each stroke.

With the strange sensations from the whip in her pussy, the warm sun on her body and a hot hard cock in her mouth Jiggles squirmed with joy. She tipped over into orgasm even faster than normal, squeezing her knees together and holding her hands in place with Edna deep inside her.

Montana paused his thrusts in and out of her mouth, surprised by her ecstasy. "That was quick."

"Edna is a wonderful lover." Jiggles told him when she'd removed his penis from her mouth. After a moment's thought she asked, "Would you like to take her place?"

Jiggles eased the whip handle out and laid it gently aside. As Montana stood and started to move around behind her she lithely flipped over onto all fours.

Her thighs were twitching with happy little aftershocks, causing her rump to bounce enticingly before Montana. He laid one hand on the dimples just above her buttocks then moved it down and and spread them. With his other hand he pressed the head of his saliva slicked hard on into the cleft and moved it slowly down. For a brief moment he paused over the wrinkled hole of her anus and she thought he may ravish it as he had the night before. It would be trickier without the lubricating oil he had used in his tent, but she was willing to give it a try if he was. She shivered with joyful anticipation.

More experienced with anal play than Jiggles, Montana decided to keep his penis moving down. He introduced the deep red head to Jiggles' puffed up, sensitive and slick labia then eased it between them. Jiggles let her arms slide out ahead of her until her head lay on the blanket. She gasped and groaned and ground against Montana's cock, encouraging him.

Montana had planned to go slow, to tease Jiggles and drive her wild. But he didn't need to, she was already writhing under him, urging him to pump hard and fast into her. He grasped her waist and held her tight as he pushed faster and faster into her.

They came together, shouting out in triumph. Jiggles pressed her forehead to the blanket as she panted and sighed with the aftershocks. Montana threw his head back and mouthed "Oh yeah." as her pussy milked the last of the semen from his sensitive cock.

As the tingles and twitches died down, something made Montana open his eyes and look around, slowly scanning as far left to right as he could. "I hope you're an exhibitionist, Miss Jiggleswick."

Jiggles twisted to look up at Montana. "Sorry?" she questioned. Then she too looked around.

There weren't many of them, but there were enough to be ominous. A small semi circle of Bedouin stood around them, twenty or thirty feet away. Oddly, they didn't look as if they had been acting as voyeurs- they hardly seemed moved at all by the display they had just seen- and Jiggles found the disappointment overrode any sense of danger.

* * *

Eustace surveyed the damage with disgust. When the raiding party had come under fire it had replied with mortar and cannon. Neither had been at all effective, the cannon had mostly fired short or wide whilst the mortar crews had thrown their shells too far. Most of the over shots had landed in or around the main pit of the archaeological dig. None of them had been a direct hit, but they had caused enough damage to collapse the giant stone slab in the main pit.

The slab was to have been removed carefully, revealing – hopefully- the grand chamber of a burial or temple complex. The raiding party had been after the ancient secrets which were now buried under the rubble. "Idiots!" raged Eustace, "Idiots!" He kicked at the remnants of a bucket, but rather than sending it tumbling into the hole he split it and sprayed dust around.

Quince was standing behind Eustace, beside a thin man in perfectly cut civilian clothes who nonetheless was the one all the troops answered to. The thin man let out a low tut and pulled a packet of cigarettes from his suit's inside pocket. He turned the packet onto its side and tapped it so that a slim cigarette popped out. He put it to his mouth and had it halfway back to the pocket when he remembered Quince.

"Would you care for a cigarette?" the thin man asked Quince. His voice was almost accent free. If anything it was too precise, a little too perfect.

German, Quince thought. "No, thank you. I'm more of a pipe man myself." he answered.

"Really? I would never have guessed."

"Oh yes. There's nothing I like more at the end of the day than a nice bit of shag. Who are you anyway?"

The thin man turned slowly to face Quince. He put the cigarette packet away and pulled out a lighter- thin, naturally, and gold. "You can call me Arnold, Herr Professor."

"What are you doing here?"

Arnold lit his cigarette and took a drag on it. After he had exhaled a long curling trail of smoke he waved the cigarette in the direction of the pit. "You should ask your assistant about that. I am merely here to aid him."

Eustace was stalking back, shoulders hunched. "What sort of amateurs did you bring with you?" he growled at Arnold, "The Fuhrer will hear of this."

"I am sure he shall. Sadly the more elite squads are not available. There are.... other projects for which they are required. They will be punished appropriately for their rash reaction. After all, someone will have to dig the debris out."

"And will they find me a virgin? One with noble blood, to replace the one I brought with me?"

Quince was perplexed. When realisation finally dawned his face became a jowly mask of shock. "Fiona?"

"Of course Fiona. I couldn't possibly mean those two sluts who flew us here. If this is to work, if we are to harness the weather control powers of the old line, then we will need a virgin sacrifice with royal blood. Fiona's family line has been watered down, but they have royalty in their past. Not that it matters now that she's buried under all that stone."

Quince was recovering his composure, but still somewhat flustered. "You don't truly believe all that nonsense about the weather control do you?"

"Why not? This whole valley...." Eustace waved his hand at the barren scenery, "was green once. They made this valley bloom."

"Smith has a theory about that."

"Smith is an idiot! He's too busy fornicating and looking for fame to see the truth. I shall harness the power of the Valley of the Wizards for the only ruler in the world strong enough to know what to do with it."

Quince turned to Arnold. "Do you believe this?" he asked.

Arnold made a small Teutonic shrug. "The Fuhrer believes it, and I am following his orders. So I do what is asked of me, to see what comes of it. Now, if you will excuse us, we must go and tell the soldiers to start digging." Arnold gestured to Eustace and they started to walk away.

"What am I supposed to do?" Quince asked loudly.

"If you can stay out of our way you are quite welcome to walk around." Arnold gestured around the valley, echoing Eustace. "Or you could wander off and try to find help."

* * *

Fiona, of course, wasn't dead. Indeed, if anyone had asked she would have told them she had never felt so alive. She was wandering the halls of an ancient tomb- something she had wanted to do ever since she started studying archaeology- practically naked, with a gorgeous woman who had taught her all sorts of things about her desires. She was having an adventure better than any of the ones she had read about in her books.

They now had two lamps to light their way. They couldn't see very far out of the flickering pool of light, and the dancing flames did their eyes' adjustment to the dark no favours. Even within the small area that was illuminated there were deep shadows which kept hiding anything from statues to doorways. So, when a very realistic hawk-headed statue appeared around a pillar, Fiona squealed- all the pent up excitement and fear getting a release- and fumbled her lamp.

"Sorry." Fiona squeaked as she bent to pick the lamp up. She paused. There was something different about the way the flames were dancing. She crouched down to get a closer look.

"Is something wrong?" Ally asked.

"No. We may have found something interesting." Fiona picked the lamp up, but held the burning end close to the floor and moved it around. As she saw the small flames jump and change direction when they passed some invisible barrier Ally began to understand what Fiona had noticed. Fiona continued, almost as if she were talking to herself, "I have never been in a freshly opened tomb before, so I didn't notice it at first. But somewhere that has been sealed up for thousands of years should be..." she looked round at Ally as she searched for the right word, "stale. It should smell of... death. And abandonment. These halls, the walls, everything is so ancient, except for the air."

"Like the oil in the lamps? How that hadn't hardened. You think someone has been down here recently?"

"Well, perhaps not for a few years. But certainly not as long ago as the Professor thinks. And it is so much.... tidier than you would expect." Fiona had traced the light draught across the floor to the base of the hawk headed statue. It stood on a plinth with slots on it, from which slightly colder air was flowing. Fiona waved the lamp around the base of the wall. "I was hoping for a hidden door." she sighed. She looked up at the statue, roughly sketched out by the light of Ally's lamp.

Ally stepped closer and they both held their lamps close to the statue and studied it. Apart from the hawk head mask- and being eight feet tall and gilded- it was a beautifully formed female nude with its arms crossed in front of, but not completely hiding, its firm conical breasts. "They're almost as good as yours." Ally commented, holding her lamp up high.

Fiona was looking at a different part of the statue. Where the tops of its thighs met, the statue's pudenda bulged gently out, emphasising the slit of her vagina. Unlike the clean vertical line of a classical European nude this one was more anatomically correct, the orchid shaped labia lips folding over and around the nub of the clitoris. Fiona reached out to gently stroke it. She realised Ally was watching her and flushed slightly, but didn't stop feeling up the statue.

Ally reached her free hand through the slit side of Fiona's dungarees, stroked a breast and tweaked its nipple. Fiona bit her lower lip and hissed. "Maybe we should move on and see if we can find a door. There must be a series of tunnels or something which this air is flowing through."

"Maybe we should." Ally moved closer and they kissed.

Their tongues probed and played with each other as they pressed closer together. Fiona stopped running her fingers over the smooth swirls of the carved labia lips and went searching for the real things. Ally twisted enough to allow access to the bow on her trousers. Fiona released it quickly, she was becoming adept at that sort of thing. Ally shimmied and the trousers fell to her ankles. Her fingers were busy as well, finding the fasteners which held Fiona's dungarees up and separating them.

Fiona's fingers played over Ally's knickers then snuck inside them. Her dungarees had dropped and pooled around her feet. Now Ally reached inside Fiona's knickers. She played her fingers through Fiona's pubic hair and moved down to her slick pussy lips. Each knowing what the other wanted they both slid an index finger easily into the other.

Ally wanted to use both hands, so she had to find somewhere to put her lamp. Breaking the kiss she looked around for one of the many wall mounts they had spotted at regular intervals in the hall. Now it was her turn to squeal in shock. She tried to take a step backwards only to trip over her own trousers.

As she fell, her hand clasped around the material of Fiona's underwear, tearing it off her.

Fiona echoed Ally's scream and staggered back to be tripped by her own clothing as well. They sat opposite each other, dazed. Before Fiona had to ask Ally raised her lamp and pointed it down the hallway. Fiona lifted her light as well, and shivered at what was revealed.

Just on the edge of the light from their lamps was a life size version of the naked hawk-headed statue. It had not been there earlier. Fiona and Ally both jumped when the statue raised its right arm and beckoned them to follow it before turning away.

* * *

There was a man with a pair of camels waiting for Amid and Ginge at the end of the gully. "I had one of the men get a message out." Amid announced, a little defensively, as he took the reins offered to him. At a twitch of the rope the camel made a dismissive huffing sound before lowering itself to its knees. "It would be best if you are to ride with me." Amid told Ginge. "I am not the best camel rider, but I imagine I have more experience than you."

Ginge balanced himself behind Amid and, uncertain what else to hang on to, wrapped his arms around his companion's waist. The other man mounted up and urged his steed to its feet in a move that almost looked graceful. Amid and Ginge's camel, on the other hand, swayed and grunted and almost threw them off.

They had only been moving for a minute when Ginge started to feel seasick. "You have a lot of explaining to do." he groaned.

"It is only fair." Amid agreed. "Where to begin?" He mused on his own question for a while, before continuing, "Do you remember yesterday I said that I was involved in the dig to find out whether my mother's tales of our family's royal lineage were true?"

"Yes."

"Well, I lied. I know I am descended from kings. My family has no power any more, but we are duty bound to defend the country and its secrets. To keep some of its secrets.... secret. The Valley of the Wizards may hold some of the biggest secrets, so I volunteered to watch over the dig and see what, if anything, was discovered."

"Such as what?"

"It is hard to say. But the wizards the valley is named for were reputed to have control over the elements, enough to make the desert bloom. I believe Doctor Smith's theory- that they harnessed advanced irrigation techniques- is more likely, but you never know. It seems others believed the legends as well and would like to have them for themselves."

"They looked like Europeans, but I didn't recognise the uniforms."

"Germans, most likely. It seems the Nazis are keen to find arcane objects and ancient secrets to harness any power they have. I have heard that they are all over the world seeking out lost cities and hidden treasures. Doctor Smith has tangled with them on a number of occasions."

"It would have been nice if you had told us all this earlier, you know."

"I would be a poor guardian of my country's secrets if I told everyone I was secretly a guardian of my nation's secrets." Amid mused.

"Well, that makes sense. I think."

They were on flatter ground now, and a whistle from the man on the leading camel signalled the transition to a gallop. Ginge decided not to ask any more questions and just hold on tight.

* * *

A shorter man, wearing finer clothes, waved the other Bedouin away. "You speak English, yes?" he asked, tactfully averting his eyes to watch the waves on the lake.

"Yes." Montana had collected Jiggles' clothes and handed them to her. They were dressing, but not too quickly, they didn't want to look as spooked as they felt.

"We saw your machine," the stranger gestured to the Hawker Hooligan, "drop out of the sky and felt it good to investigate. I am happy to see you are very alive."

Jiggles buttoned up her blouse. "Thank you. Did you....?"

"It would have been impolite to interrupt. I must assure you we hid behind the rise until you were finished."

"That was most gallant of you." Montana commented as he buttoned up his trousers. "Montana Smith. And this is Miss Veronica Jiggleswick, the pilot and owner of the airplane. Who do we have the pleasure of addressing?"

"I am Mustafa. My caravan is but a short way around the lake. I can offer you my hospitality for the rest of the day and the night, whilst my men recover your craft."

"That would be lovely." Jiggles admitted.

"Very good. Please come this way, we have horses."

The horses were gorgeous creatures. Many of Jiggles' friends had built up equine collections in their childhoods- just as young ladies should- whilst she had become fascinated by aviation. She had never had her own horse, but had ridden enough to know that the four pure white stallions, with highly decorated bridles and saddles, were of a fine pedigree. A young man was sat on one of the horses holding the reins of the other three. He brought them forward as Jiggles, Montana and Mustafa walked down the slope.

"Father." The youngster handed the reins to Mustafa. He glanced at Montana then cast a lingering gaze in Jiggles' direction. "These are the strangers?" he asked.

"Mister Smith and Miss Jiggleswick." Mustafa announced as he handed them a rein each. With a practised move he climbed easily into the saddle.

Jiggles and Montana were less graceful getting into the saddle, but were seated comfortably soon enough. "This is my son Yusuf." Mustafa announced, "He has just returned from England, where he received the finest education a simple trader such as I could pay for. I am thinking he should go back, to university, to learn about politics. And maybe women."

"Father!" Yusuf had been eyeing Jiggles' form but now, embarrassed and annoyed, he looked away and urged his horse into a canter so he could pull ahead of them.

Mustafa tutted at the receding back of his son. "I really thought he would learn some carnal arts. Are English ladies really prudish?"

"Not all of them." Montana confided, with a theatrical look in Jiggles' direction.

Mustafa pondered this for a moment before abruptly changing the subject. "Are you with the diggers in the Valley of the Wizards?"

"We are. We came up here to search for more sites to investigate." Montana replied.

"And your flying machine broke?"

"I think it was sabotaged." Jiggles piped up. She turned in her saddle, "I think someone doctored the fuel. We shall know for sure when I get a chance to look at the fuel lines."

"My men will leave that part of the machine alone. But they will move it, and attempt to clear a take off strip for you. There was damage to the..." Mustafa rotated a finger in the air, trying sum up the word he was thinking of.

"The wheel. One of the wheels." Jiggles offered.

"Yes, yes, the wheel. It has damage. They may be able to repair that, but it will take them time. So I must insist you share our hospitality whilst you wait. We shall send a rider to report your whereabouts to your friends at the dig."

They rounded a wall of rocks and were greeted by a village of tents with a hubbub of activity all around. "We never saw this from the airplane." Montana announced.

"We make camp with rapidity. This was not here when you flew over, and we were some miles away. That is why we took so long to find you, and gave you enough time to....." Mustafa let his voice trail off and grinned. "Come. We shall find food for you and you must tell me what you have found in the Valley of the Wizards."

* * *

The naked figure kept disappearing from the ring of lamp light then slowing down enough to fade back into their vision. Fiona and Ally followed as fast as they could as they were led along a memorised route through the maze of tunnels.

Eventually they came to a lightly shelving beach of flaked stone. At the water's edge sat a dhow similar to the ones which plied North Africa's rivers, crewed by two naked oarsmen and with another naked hawk-headed woman standing in the prow. Their guide talked quickly but deferentially to the older, and obviously senior, woman in the boat before bowing to her and running up a plank from the beach to the boat. Unsure of the protocol, Ally and Fiona each bowed their heads to the senior hawk before teetering up the gang plank themselves.

The younger hawk-head took Ally and Fiona's lamps and placed them in sockets above the stern. Then she motioned for them to sit on the bench the flickering light revealed. She sat on a single seat facing them and, as the oarsmen pulled in the plank and pushed away from the shore, she removed her avian helmet.

Ally's mouth fell open and she gasped. She was looking at the woman from her vision, the beauty she had imagined whilst making love to Fiona in the dark.

The girl smiled, and Ally realised she wasn't exactly the woman she had seen earlier. Her face was very slightly thinner and her lips fuller. But she had the same eyes and the similarity was uncanny. "No English." she said apologetically, then added, "Kita."

"Fiona." replied Fiona, holding a hand to her chest.

"Ally." Ally followed suit.

The boat rocked gently as the oarsmen built up a rhythm. It was impossible to judge how large the body of water they were crossing was, but the darkness swallowed the light from their lamps before it could illuminate ceiling or walls.

They sat in confused silence for a while before Fiona, brow furrowed in concentration, tried a phrase in the local dialect. Kita beamed at knowing what the beautiful foreigner was saying, and started a very animated reply. Unable to keep up Fiona leaned forward and took one of Kita's hands in both of hers and gently explained that she didn't speak the language very well. Kita looked embarrassed for a moment then laid her free hand over Fiona's and continued more slowly.

Every so often Fiona would turn to Ally to impart some more of Kita's information. "Kita is one of the temple guardians, tasked with keeping the old secrets secret. She is descended from the original temple prostitutes...."

"Temple prostitutes?"

Fiona broke off from her conversation with Kita to give a quick history lesson. "The temple prostitutes were held in high regard. They were priestesses as well; the two roles overlapped. They were revered and were the models for the naked statues." Fiona blushed slightly, remembering what they had been doing when Kita had found them. She squeezed the girl's hands and urged her to continue.

"When it became obvious that the temple would be uncovered, the guardians began removing some of the artefacts for safe keeping. They had help from within the camp, reports on progress."

"Amid." said Kita with a smile.

Fiona and Ally looked at the girl before them, then at each other. Before they could ask any more questions the roof swooped down into the torch light and another beach became obvious.

The dhow grounded on the crunchy sand and the woman in the prow called out an order before stepping down. Kita donned her hawk head and handed Ally and Fiona their lamps then led them to the front of the boat. As they stepped between the oarsmen, neither man seemed all that moved by their presence.

Ally and Fiona followed the two naked hawk-headed women into a fissure in the rock, then up steep steps hewn into a natural tunnel to make passage easier. Eventually they turned a corner into a large chamber lit by sunlight and full of attendants.

Blinded by the light, Ally and Fiona let their lamps be taken away and gentle hands guide them to a shady spot whilst their eyes adjusted.

When their vision had returned they saw a thin attendant before them. He bowed and motioned for them to follow him.

They exited another fissure and found themselves between two cliff walls. Carved into the walls were simple rooms with reed beds and seats. Some of the rooms had linen curtains which could be dropped should privacy be desired. In one of the rooms, without the curtain down, a young couple made love. An older woman stood at the back of the room making comments that could only be instructions or advice. Irrevocably changed from the shy flower who had set off from England a week before, Fiona stared at the lovers, taking mental notes.

The trench curved to the right and widened, eventually opening out into a bowl which was a natural amphitheatre. Standing at the bowl's centre were three figures. On the left was Kita, with her mask off and now wearing a demure white robe. In the middle was an older woman in a similar robe. From the way she held herself it was obvious she was the other woman from the boat. On the right was a man in a westernised outfit of rough jacket and trousers over a baggy shirt. The man spoke, "My ladies are not speaking your language, but Kita tells that you know some of ours."

"A very small amount." Fiona announced modestly in the native tongue.

The man nodded and smiled. "I will be translator for you."

"Thank you." Fiona bowed to the man and then the two women. Ally followed suit.

The older woman spoke, staring at Ally and Fiona whilst she did. Fiona understood some of what she said, but waited for the translation. "We had almost emptied temple when bomb? Yes, bomb. Goes off and breaks roof. You know who did this?"

"We were told it was raiders, thieves. But I did not see who attacked the dig. I was in the main pit at the time. Did you see anything?" The question was aimed at Ally, who answered in the negative.

"Scouts saw soldiers. European soldiers. We have heard bad tales of the warring tribes of Europe."

"We are not warring. Well, not much. Not yet." Ally offered as a weak defence.

"Kita went for you. Saved you."

"We owe her our lives. We would never have found our way out of the tunnels by ourselves. How can we repay her?"

"That is generous. But you have little to give. We ask for none." Kita tried not to look upset when she heard these words.

"We have one thing we may be able to offer." Fiona confided with a smile. She glanced at Ally, who was puzzled as to what the prize might be. "We can offer ourselves."

Kita grinned when the offer was translated, and almost jumped up and down on the spot. She turned wide eyes to the older woman, who smiled and replied, "That is generous offer. Kita is honoured to take your reward. Room will be prepared. We get you food."

Ally was staring at Fiona, surprised, and in awe, at the brazen deal she had just struck. Fiona whispered, "I hope you don't mind."

"Not at all. Not at all."

"Maybe you can explain why you were so shocked to see Kita though."

They had gained a crowd whilst talking to the two priestesses, the members of which were now busying themselves with fetching food and creature comforts. Whilst Kita talked to the older priestess Ally recounted the vision she had experienced during their earlier lovemaking, emphasising the uncanny resemblance Kita had to the woman she had seen. Fiona was intrigued, but totally at a loss for an explanation.

Kita bounced over and held out her hands to Fiona and Ally. They took one each and let her lead them back into the ravine and to their room. It was one of the larger caves, the floor liberally spread with reed mats and cushions. Kita paused at the entrance and reached for the curtain. "Closed?" she asked Fiona, who gave it a moment's thought before admitting that she wasn't yet that daring and nodding.

The curtain was light enough to allow decent illumination. After the pitch black of the temple anything was bright, if now a little monochrome. The three women stood on the reeds and looked each other up and down.

Fiona was the first to disrobe, for her it was just a matter of releasing a few buttons. When she clasped her hands behind her back and presented her naked form to Ally and Kita they both made appreciative noises. Ally motioned that Kita should act on her barely concealed desires. The dark beauty stepped forward and tentatively reached out to touch the pale, smooth skin of Fiona's up-tilted breasts. She swirled a finger up the cone of Fiona's left breast then gently tweaked the tight nipple.

Ally had spotted that Kita's robe was held together by buttons which ran all the way down its back and started releasing them slowly and tantalisingly. When they were undone she ran a finger down Kita's spine, raising a purr. Fiona gently took the shorter woman's chin in her hand and lifted it up to kiss her. As their lips locked and tongues played Ally took the opportunity to slide the robe from Kita's shoulders and reveal her gorgeous nakedness again.

Kita and Fiona kissed passionately, pressed hard against each other and rubbed flesh against flesh. Ally watched them with awe. She wasn't the slightest bit jealous, the view was far too erotic to get green eyed about. Or keep out of.

Ally stepped close to Kita and Fiona, though they didn't seem to notice. She reached out her hands and ran fingers down each of their spines. Now they noticed. When she reached the base of their backs she grasped buttock cheeks. Kita's were fuller than Fiona's, but just as firm. They turned to face Ally as she squeezed their bums and took it in turns to kiss her.

Pulling in even closer to Kita and Fiona, Ally's fingers moved further around to tease at two sets of wet pussy lips. She couldn't get much of her fingers' length in, but it had the desired effect. Kita and Fiona looked at each other then turned to Ally. Fiona started unfastening her top whilst Kita knelt before her to remove her trousers.

In a trice Ally was as naked as her companions. She looked down at Kita, who was beaming with joy and lust, then across at Fiona, flushed with desire. Fiona reached down and urged Kita to stand again. "This is for you." she announced, "What do you wish?"

Kita appeared flustered at having to make a decision. Her reply confused Fiona, who had to ask for an explanation. Kita thought some more, before pointing at her crotch and trying to explain in simpler language. Fiona nodded, thinking she understood. "Kita would like us to taste her...." She too pointed at Kita's genital region, a trace of her old shyness returning. "Can you show me how it is done?" she asked, "I have never done that before."

"With pleasure." Ally replied. She leaned in and kissed Kita, turning her as she did.

Fiona tried to explain what they had agreed, as best she could. Kita pulled away from Ally, grinning, and started explaining a different plan in rapid fire and illustrating it with gestures. The hand movements and the way she ushered Fiona over to the largest of the cushions helped make her plan obvious.

Fiona dropped onto the cushion and shuffled around until she was comfortable, making sure that her feet were widely spaced and flat on the floor. She put her hands on her knees and held those apart as well, spreading her thighs and displaying her pussy. Kita and Ally ogled the display then shared a look. Kita was on her knees again in a moment. She hustled forwards and hooked her arms under Fiona's thighs.

Ally had wanted to be the one to introduce Fiona to the joys of a tongue playing on her private parts- gamahuching as her great aunt Gertie used to call it. The eccentric old spinster had always had a happy far away look when she used the word and it was at moments like this that Ally understood why. The momentary twinge of jealousy was wiped away with a glance at the tense joy on Fiona's face and the gentle swaying of Kita's buttocks as she kissed up and down milky white thighs. Ally lay on her back between Kita's legs then shuffled toward her pussy on shoulders and feet.

Fiona's hands slid down from her knees to rest on Kita's head. She ran her fingers through the girl's jet black hair, massaging her scalp. Kita switched from one thigh to the other and Fiona squeaked and giggled. She so wanted to press the other woman's head down to her hot sensitive labia lips, but she resisted. Kita knew what she was doing, and Fiona was eager to learn from her.

As Kita dipped her head to flick her tongue out and tease Fiona's lips her hips lifted. Ally tutted as Kita's hot pussy moved away from her. She sat up so she could glue her lips to it, pushing her tongue deep inside. Kita made a happy ululation and pressed her lips down on Fiona. From the way Fiona started squirming it seemed Kita had carried on singing.

Ally wrapped an arm around Kita's waist so she could hold on tight as her talented tongue did its work. Kita passed the pleasure on to Fiona who, despite her desire to watch and learn, couldn't help but throw her head back, close her eyes and give voice to her ecstasy.

Kita came first, but hardly paused her licking of Fiona even as her thighs clasped tight but shivering about Ally's head. Fiona couldn't help herself any more and held Kita's head in place, guiding the tongue inside her. She started gyrating her hips against Kita's tongue as she drew closer and closer to orgasm. Her cries were loud and unrestrained. That she could feel such pleasure, and express it so freely, was a revelation even to her.

With a scream that drew appreciative glances from those on the outside of the cave, Fiona came.

"Oh my." Fiona managed to sigh out, some time later. She hadn't moved from the pillow, but she didn't want to, not with Kita curled up in her lap and playing fingers over her still twitching belly.

Ally sat across from them, cross-legged on a small pillow she had pulled up. She drank in the tableau the other two women formed. Kita's dark skin was in stark contrast to Fiona's peachy white, and her womanly curves more pronounced than those of Fiona's willowy slim body. Just the sight of the two of them turned her on, and her right hand began unconsciously stroking at the insides of her thighs then up to the curve of her belly as it tucked in toward her vagina lips. She ran fingers through her dark, tight pubic hair, parting it and playing with it, before moving below it.

Her pussy lips were so sensitive that she let out a sigh just from running fingers down either side of of them. She gently wagged her forefinger back and forth over the lips, so close that every couple of sweeps she rubbed gently against them, raising twitches in her thighs. As Ally's gaze moved up again she realised that Fiona was watching her.

Fiona leaned down to whisper in Kita's ear and the other woman roused with a smile. She slid from Fiona's lap and stalked toward Ally on all fours, almost cat like in the sway of her hips and the arch of her back. Ally froze and held her breath. She had been satisfied to have given this dark beauty- and, indirectly, Fiona – pleasure, and hadn't been expecting any more sex to happen. Kita cocked her head when she reached Ally and started kissing her gently. Each kiss was a little peck, with just enough pressure to urge Ally slowly back, onto Kita's supporting arm, then down to the floor.

With Kita's tongue in her mouth and hands on her breasts, Ally almost didn't notice the gentle hands on her calves. Slim fingers wrapped around her ankles and moved them to unhook and spread her legs. Lost in a reverie of Kita's attentions it took Ally a while to realise what was happening. Fiona, her beautiful and- until recently- timid and pure English rose, was about to go down on her. She wanted to dig her heels into the floor, lever her hips off the floor and lift her pussy to Fiona's lips, but resisted. They would come to her soon enough.

Kita kissed all around Ally's face, then down her neck and up one then the other breast. Ally almost didn't know that her nipples were being alternately nibbled and sucked, she was too focussed on what had yet to happen between her legs. She stared at the ceiling, trying to relax but constantly imagining and re-imagining what was to happen next and getting ever more excited as she did.

Fiona had her fingers gently resting on the insides of Ally's knees as she stared at the wavy lips of Ally's pussy. They darkened as they engorged and folded open without even being touched. She could smell the musky, erotic aroma of Ally's excitement. Mesmerised, Fiona had frozen in place. The sound of Kita's enthusiastic licking and slurping around Ally's breasts- and the low moan Ally probably didn't realise she was making- reminded her of the task in hand.

Fiona's fingers started travelling up Ally's thighs, aiming for her pussy. The moan changed pitch and became more of a series of low pants. Fiona stopped her hands just short of the prize, prompting a whimper from Ally, then moved them quickly around and up to Ally's hips. Using her hand holds to help,

Fiona pulled herself up to plant a hasty kiss on Ally's pussy lips. "Ooya!" Ally exclaimed. Kita's head popped up from Ally's perfect hemisphere breasts and she looked around, a little confused. When she saw where Fiona's face was she simply smiled and returned to her ministrations.

Fiona studied the hot, slick lips before her. She sniffed the heady erotic aroma then sneaked out a tongue and licked at them to taste their delicious tangy flavour. She didn't know what her actions were doing to Ally, but she could feel her own orgasm mounting. It was selfish, but she sneaked one hand back to push two, then three, fingers into her own wet pussy. With the other hand she spread Ally's labia so she could sneak her tongue in deeper.

Ally had grasped two handfuls of matting and was squeezing them tight until her fingers went white. Fiona's tongue flicked at her clitoris and she let out a happy "Oooh." With some effort she relaxed the hand nearest Kita and walked the fingers across the floor until they encountered smooth skin. Kita understood perfectly what the questing hand was looking for. She moved around and opened her legs so that Ally's fingers could climb up her thigh and find the opening of her quim. She clasped the hand, with two of its fingers inside her, between her thighs and rotated against it.

The three of them were each heading rapidly towards climax now. Ally lifted one then the other leg onto Fiona's shoulders, crossing her feet at the ankles. Kita sat up and quickly moved to straddle Ally's face, leaning forwards to kiss Fiona across the shoulders and Ally on the knees. As Ally began flicking her tongue into Kita, Fiona began thrusting two fingers into Ally. The room filled with happy little gasps, panted breaths and soft squelches.

Ally came first, her cries muffled between Kita's thighs. She didn't stop lapping at the cunny lips which pressed down on her, even going so far as to grasp Kita's thighs and hold her in place whilst redoubling her oral efforts. This brought the dark beauty to orgasm even quicker. Kita cried out unknown words of joy as her body shook and shimmied. Last, but never ever least, Fiona's own fingers- on top of the sensory overload from the other women's climaxes- pushed her over the edge.

They lay in satiated bliss upon the matting for a while, until the comfort of the pile of cushions beckoned them. Too shaky to stand, they crawled over, kissing areas of flesh that swayed too close. Kita nested in the indentation Fiona had left in the larger cushion and Fiona and Ally curled up either side of her.

Hands explored, and there were more kisses, but they had too little energy for another round and drifted off to dream of dark tunnels where naked gods roamed and glorious orgies took place.

* * *

The camels slowed as the land sloped upwards. They followed the pale yellow trail of a recently travelled path as it switched back and forth up a slope and over a ridge. The rise formed a bowl around a mustard yellow cliff face with two large slabs of rock propped against it. Their guide stopped beside the rocks and dismounted.

Once again, Ginge was nearly thrown from the saddle as the camel knelt down to let him off. When he was safely on the ground again he turned away from Amid and their guide and reached down the front of his trousers to check on the state of his testicles and Little Ginge. Satisfied his package was still in one piece, he walked around the camel and surveyed the area.

They were well hidden in their natural amphitheatre, but he couldn't see why else they were in it. Then someone walked out of the gap between the stones. She was a short and attractive dark skinned woman in a light white dress. She looked annoyed as she walked up to Amid. Stopping short of him she looked him up and down and said, with a sigh, "Cousin." Before Amid could reply she slapped him. "Kita was in the temple when the attack happened." she declared.

"I'm sure your sister will be alright." Amid replied, reaching up to touch his smarting cheek.

"The temple roof collapsed. She may not have been inside when it happened, but I do not know for certain." The woman turned to Ginge. "You are English?" she asked. Ginge nodded. "I chose to speak your language, so you would understand. Some of the workers who were there when the raid happened told that there were two English women on the temple roof before it collapsed."

"Ally and Fiona." Ginge gasped. "Oh no."

"Like my sister, we do not know yet what happened to them. But I am sorry, you must be prepared for the worst." There was sadness in the woman's big brown eyes as she turned back to Amid. "You are alive and well?" she asked. When he nodded she hugged him. "You must introduce me to your friend."

"I have been rude. This is my step-cousin Sorya, she works with the temple prostitutes. They were making sure there was nothing too.... revealing in the temple. Sorya, this is Ginge. He arrived at the dig yesterday with his companions."

Sorya studied Ginge more closely. "You are intimate with my cousin?" she asked.

Still trying to comprehend the possible loss of Ally and Fiona- and still wondering what had happened to Jiggles and Montana- Ginge could only stammer, "I.... have been. Not.... not right now, obviously."

"Come. I shall tell you what we are doing to combat these grave robbers, and how we shall avenge our losses." Sorya turned and walked back through the crack in the rocks. Amid and Ginge followed. The guide mounted his camel and rode off, leading the other away.

Through the gap a crack in the cliff continued further back than Ginge would have expected. There was a large low hammock, wide enough to be a double bed, slung between the walls, and space had been cleared for cooking and eating areas. A kettle bubbled on a small brass camp stove and a folding table was piled with bread. Sorya sat beside the stove and poured boiling water into a pot. "The English adore tea, I hear." she said, "This may not be the sort you are used to."

"Thank you." They sat in silence as the leaves steeped, each pondering the day's developments in silence. When Sorya was finally satisfied with the look of the brew she poured it out into glass cups so small they were practically thimbles. Ginge took the offered drink and sipped it. It was crisp and left a tingle then a soothing warmth over his tongue and then down his throat. He knocked back the rest of the tiny cup then held it out for a refill.

"I must warn you," Sorya said as she held up the pot, "that this is a tea to warm the, ah, sexual parts. It is all I brought, as I thought I would be alone for some days."

Ginge considered the aphrodisiac qualities of this refreshing drink, and kept the cup held out for a refill. Amid shrugged and offered up his glass for more as well.

Four cups later, Ginge was beginning to feel the warmth in his groin. His penis wasn't hard, but it did feel engorged, hot and sensitive where it lay against his thigh. The arousal was nearly enough to take his mind away from fears for his friends' lives. Much more and he'd happily indulge himself, no matter how guilty he felt later. With the luck that favoured the horny, he soon wouldn't have to feel bad in the morning.

There was a voice from the cave entrance, their guide calling for Sorya's attention. She blinked half closed eyelids open as her name was repeated, then stood up, uncurling from the cushion in a most erotic manner. In her current state she couldn't help but sashay across the floor with rolling hips and round, firm buttocks moving seductively inside her gown. Amid and Ginge stared at her progress across the dusty floor, trapped erections pushing at the material of their trousers.

Sorya conversed with the guide for a few moments, asking for details of the news he brought. Finally she thanked him and sent him on his way. Sorya spun on her heels and smiled. Her movements as she returned to the cushions were, if possible, more alluring. "My men have seen a message from the main encampment. They report that all the priestesses got out of the caves safely, and Kita brought two white women with her. There are also reports that an airplane has landed by the great lake. It was forced down but did not crash. It seems, mister Ginge, that all of your friends, and ours, are alive and well."

"That is such great news!" Ginge tried to stand, but his stiff and sensitive penis made him wince as it rubbed against his trouser leg. He self consciously reached down to see if he could rearrange it.

Sorya stood over Ginge. Her full breasts strained at the material of her dress, their long, stiff nipples threatening to tear little holes in it. "Did I not tell you of the effects my tea could have."

"I was warned." Ginge said with a smile.

Turning to her step-cousin, Sorya asked, "You have seen his penis? Is it as magnificent as this bulge in mister Ginge's trousers promises?"

"It is a wonderful freckled beast." Amid assured her.

Sorya's hands had been resting on her hips and, seemingly unconsciously, bunching up the cotton of her dress so that the hem was now most of the way up her thighs. Amid and Ginge only now noticed this and were entranced by the slowly rising line of material. "If you could help release the beast cousin. Whilst I disrobe."

Amid's eager hands went straight to the belt and buttons of Ginge's trousers. Ginge sat back and let Amid do all the work, so that he could watch Sorya slowly draw her dress up.

A thin triangle of white cotton hid Sorya's quim from sight, though the material was moulded so closely to her body that it might as well not have been there. As the skirt lifted higher, Ginge spotted the thin straps that held the fabric in place, each tied with a little bow. He was thinking about reaching out and undoing them just as Amid pulled his trousers down and released Little Ginge. Sorya paused and studied the fine erection with a smile. Spurred on by the promise of the freckled monster, she tugged the dress quickly over her head and tossed it aside.

Amid had almost removed Ginge's pants, but he stopped to stare up at Sorya's magnificent nearly naked form. He had seen, and enjoyed, it before, but it always merited studying. She may have been short, but she was exquisitely formed- shapely legs, full round buttocks, slim waist and large firm breasts- their long hard nipples pointing almost straight up at the ceiling. Sorya smirked and nodded at Ginge's trousers, urging Amid to finish the job he had started. The trousers were off in a flash.

As Sorya knelt before the now half naked Ginge Amid stood to strip off his own clothes. Sorya placed her hands either side of Ginge's thighs, letting her long black hair hang down to tickle around his testicles and cock. "It has a.... sheath." she mused upon seeing the foreskin.

"I know." mumbled Amid, muffled by the shirt he was trying to pull off without unbuttoning. He was attempting to step out of his trousers as well, but failed and fell over sideways. Neither Sorya nor Ginge paid any attention to the slapstick. She was watching his hard on quiver with pent up excitement, breathing hard on it. He was watching her, waiting for her to stop panting and start kissing.

Sorya's head dipped even closer, and angled so she could nibble the underside of Ginge's erection. Her lips teased just below the head then worked their way down to the wrinkled sack that held his balls. A talented tongue hooked under a tender ovoid and pulled it into her mouth. As Sorya sucked the testicle Ginge made a small nervous but excited sound. Her teeth caught the ball oh-so-gently. It was still enough to send a thrill of erotic terror through Ginge.

As turned on as he was, Ginge was still pleased when Sorya set his testicle free and looked up to where Amid stood beside them. "Always impressive, cousin." she purred as she reached out a hand to cup his balls. She moved aside, so that she was on Ginge's right, and motioned to Amid. "Join me." she suggested. Amid dropped quickly to his knees and almost immediately had his lips around the head of Ginge's cock.

"Do not be so greedy." Sorya chided. Amid released Ginge's hard on and Sorya took his place. Amid started licking up and down what little of the shaft Sorya had not swallowed. Ginge just kept repeating "Oh yes." very quietly.

Sorya released Ginge's erection when she was sure she and Amid had sucked and licked him as hard as he was going to get. It was obvious she was taking the lead. Ginge vaguely wondered if this was how their relationship always worked. Then Amid gave his cock a goodbye lick from balls to head, and he didn't really care any more.

"Mister Ginge. If you will come this way." Sorya offered Ginge her hand and helped him stand with surprising strength. When he was shakily on his feet she unbuttoned his shirt and pushed it off. Meanwhile, Amid had retrieved a familiar object, a small brass jug with a thin S-shaped spout. He tipped it to pour out some of the super slick lubricating oil he and Ginge had used the night before. He swirled his fingers around, enjoying the sensation, and grinned.

Sorya guided Ginge over to the hammock and made him lie in it. It immediately started swaying, so he planted his feet on the floor and tried to stop the movement. He watched as Sorya's hands went to her thong. She took the ends of each bow between thumb and forefinger and gently tugged them. Oh so slowly the bows shrank, then pulled through, and the knot unravelled. The back of her thong dropped down, but she held the front up so that the panel still hid her pubis. She waved the material from side to side then dropped it. Her pussy lips, as promised, bulged out, undulating over each other as they swept up to the hood over her prominent clitoris.

Amid knelt down behind Sorya, running his free hand over her buttocks. He poured the oil between her buttocks and then over his fingers. As Ginge watched and waited, Sorya ran her hands through her long black hair and lifted it up into horns above her head. When the strands had run through her fingers they dropped haphazardly over and around her face. She kept her hands lifted high, knitting her fingers together and staring up at them.

Amid slid a lubricated finger into the tight puckered hole of Sorya's behind and she let out a low moan of pleasure. Ginge figured out what Amid and Sorya were working towards and grasped the edge of the hammock excitedly. Amid poured out more lubricant and squeezed a second finger into Sorya's bottom. Her hips rotated and swayed back and forth, moving the fingers inside her. She lifted her breasts then stroked and teased them before pinching her nipples hard. Amid paused from thrusting his fingers into Sorya to pass the jug through her legs to Ginge.

Ginge dribbled oil onto his hard on then swirled it around and all over the organ, until it glistened. He looked up at Sorya and they nodded to each other that they were ready.

At a word from Sorya, Amid stood up. Sorya turned around so her fine buttocks were visible to Ginge. Guided by Amid, she started shuffling backwards. He held her arms and took her weight as she began lowering herself toward Little Ginge. Ginge reached up and cupped a firm buttock cheek in each hand, separating them and revealing her lubricated and waiting arsehole.

When the deep red head of his penis lodged between Sorya's buttocks and started sliding up and down the cleft Ginge brought a hand round to help guide it. He held it on target as Sorya bore gently down on it. She relaxed, as much as possible in the situation, and the wrinkled ring of muscle opened around the head.

With Ginge and Amid to help her, Sorya slid slowly down Ginge's hard on. All three of them gasped as the fat head popped past her sphincter. With that hurdle cleared Sorya's progress was easier and smoother. She kept on bearing down until Ginge was fully lodged inside her backside. Amid let her go and she lay back on Ginge's chest and stretched her legs out over his. He reached around and squeezed and massaged her fine breasts and stiff, sensitive nipples.

The muscles of Sorya's back passage worked on Ginge's erection, making him move his hips to try to drive it in and out, even if only a short distance. He reached a hand down to play it up and down the curved labia lips and around the protruding clitoris. Sorya wriggled in response, passing the excitement back to Ginge.

Amid was on his knees before Sorya and Ginge, holding his hard on and steadying his aim. Ginge reached out and grabbed the dark cock. He tugged it closer and rubbed the head through Sorya's closely trimmed pubic hair then teased it at her clitoris. She liked this, and her response meant he liked it too. Ginge began running Amid's penis up and down Sorya's slick lips, teasing them apart and then guiding it between them.

With the head of Amid's cock inside his step-cousin's pussy, Ginge let it go. Amid slid easily into Sorya, pressing his hard on against the back wall of her vagina and feeling Ginge pushing back. The three of them groaned in unison. Amid kissed Sorya and then Ginge before starting to thrust in and out.

Amid's movements set the hammock swinging, which messed up Ginge's rhythm. He stopped trying to follow and just lay back and enjoyed the ride. Sorya's back passage grasped him tight, squeezing and massaging his cock, and he could feel each of Amid's movements inside her. He didn't have to do anything and he was still helping drive the woman atop him wild.

Ginge could feel his climax building. He clenched his buttocks, trying to hold it in but knowing he was fighting a losing battle. Biting his lower lip and grasping the hammock tight he managed a few more of Amid's thrusts before pumping semen deep inside Sorya. He couldn't relax completely once the twitching stopped, he was always sensitive just after he came and he could feel all of Amid's continuing moves as exquisite spasms in his cock. He let his body relax, as much as was possible, and let the sensations roll over him.

Taking advantage of the change of pace, Amid lifted Sorya's legs and hooked the knees over his shoulders. This changed the angle he pushed into her and, as he rocked back and forth, moved Sorya's arse further up and down Ginge's cock. It was all so intense on Ginge's tender hard on that he couldn't help but whimper under them. Amid pushed on and on, building and building to his climax. Sorya cried out as she peaked and shook with an orgasm that shivered through all three of them. Ginge, to his surprise, found that he'd gone through the exquisite pain and was once again approaching orgasm.

Ginge didn't think he had anything left to pump into Sorya, but he came again, calling out with a shout she matched. Amid held himself deep inside his step-cousin and made the cries a three part harmony. He released Sorya's legs and collapsed onto her chest. The hammock's swings slowed and eventually stopped whilst its occupants breathed deeply and let out happy sighs.

* * *

Mustafa's hospitality was very distracting. For one who claimed to be a simple trader he did have a surfeit of luxuries in his tent and a large entourage. He had even, it appeared, brought along some of his concubines, for those cold desert nights. "I have two wives." he explained, "One at either end of the trade route. It is not that they hate each other. But my life is so much calmer when they do not have to meet. The young ladies who accompany us are often looking for safe passage and sometimes they make payment in kind."

"What exactly do you trade in?" Montana asked. He had been doing mental arithmetic based upon the number of horses and camels he had seen and the logistics of transporting such a large camp and several ladies of easy virtue.

"Not the ladies." Mustafa answered hastily, "They travel of their own accord and for their own benefit. No. If I tell you that there are mines of a certain sort at the landward end of my route....."

Before they could delve into the details of what sort of stones Mustafa carried or, cheekily, where he kept them, one of the caravan bosses entered the tent and addressed Mustafa in their native language. The trader raised his eyebrows, intrigued, and nodded understanding. "Most interesting." he said to Montana and Jiggles when he had finished conversing with his lieutenant, "Whilst clearing a strip for your airplane, my men have uncovered something very intriguing. I am having the horses brought around, and we shall go and investigate."

The Hooligan had been turned around and pointed back along the strip of earth it had landed on. Jiggles studied the lay of the land and tried not to show the chill that went through her when she realised how much rougher the landing could have been. When she saw the intriguing feature they had come to examine, she could hold the bravado back no more. She checked the scuffs left by the aeroplane's wheels and mused, quietly, "We were less than two feet from it."

It was two rectangular blocks of stone, each a foot wide by five long, which were about four feet apart. On the outside they stood six inches or so out of the sand, but the gap between them was much deeper. Over time it had been filled with soft sand. Two men were shovelling this out and were already four feet down. They had uncovered another two walls, lining the shaft. If the Hooligan had hit the well, or whatever it was, at this point in its landing it would have lost a wheel and cartwheeled out of control. Jiggles shivered and tried not to picture the carnage.

There was a clank from the hole, metal on stone, and a call for attention. Everyone crowded around the small hole, trying to get a better look. The diggers had hit a level of stones, jagged blocks from the size of a fist to a head, which had been thrown in to block up the hole. Without waiting for anyone to move, the diggers started tossing the stones out of the hole. They did have the sense not to throw them to the side that Mustafa stood on.

"Mister Montana, you are an archaeologist. What do you make of this?" Mustafa asked.

"Well, this close to the lake I can't rightly see it being a well. It could be a cellar for a building that used to be here." Montana leant forward to stare into the hole, though in truth he couldn't see anything beyond the two men throwing stones out. "But, really, I reckon we'll find a secret room or some such."

"Do you think there shall be treasure?" Mustafa asked. When he recognised the avarice creeping into his voice he added, "Of course, a respected archaeologist like yourself would have to document it all."

"Of course."

One of the men in the shaft stopped and shouted out. Mustafa questioned him, very interested in his reply. "They have found a gap." he announced, "Under that stone there, you see?"

"A tunnel?" Jiggles asked.

"Perhaps." Mustafa stepped away from the hole and gave out a series of instructions. The men around them, and the two in the hole, set about their assigned tasks. "It will take them several more hours to empty this hole. They will continue for some time tonight and start again in the morning. We shall go and eat."

Montana and Mustafa started toward the horses. Jiggles stood by the hole, watching as more bricks came flying out, then had to jog to catch up. "I just noticed, your son isn't with us." she said to Mustafa when she caught up.

"No. I believe my comments earlier, they were maybe too embarrassing to him and he is trying his luck with one of the young ladies at the camp. I hope it is not too expensive."

Yusuf was sat outside the main tent, puffing on a hookah pipe. He had a faraway look, whether from the narcotic smoke he was bubbling through the brass contraption, or a successfully negotiated assignation, couldn't be determined yet. He still gave Jiggles an appreciative look over as she dismounted. He stood to bow a greeting to his father and then to Jiggles and Montana. "The meal is ready father. And some of the young ladies have promised us a.... show."

"Really?" Mustafa grinned, "Well, we should eat then. Come my honoured guests, let us eat."

*　*　*

As it started getting dark Quince had taken a seat and a bag to the highest point in the camp. He had found a bottle of Montana Smith's bourbon and he intended to drink it all. Behind him the main hole of the dig site was lit up as the soldiers tried to dig through the collapsed masonry whilst Eustace lorded it over them.

The obnoxious young twit had tried lecturing Quince about the multitudinous excellent qualities of Herr Hitler and why National Socialism was the only answer for the world. Quince hadn't wasted any energy explaining how much he was wrong and how evil the ideology he espoused was. Rather, he had simply turned his back on his former pupil and walked away.

It was all a terrible, terrible mess. He had stopped worrying about the damage to his reputation at about the same time as his head had stopped hurting where Eustace had cold cocked him with a revolver. His good name was long gone. The whole horrible thing in the country house the year before was going to follow him around for the rest of his days. He had been a fool to think that getting involved with a high profile dig might bolster his credibility.

Now all he could worry about was just what damage these barbarians might do with anything they found under the ground. He didn't believe there was any supernatural secret to the Valley of the Wizards, but Eustace and his Nazi friends did, and were willing to kill to get it. The workers had taken their dead and wounded with them as they set out into the desert, so Quince couldn't know how many had already perished in the name of this damn fool quest. The archaeology students were being kept under guard in their tents, about as safe in the long run as Quince himself was.

Then there was poor young Fiona and her friend, buried somewhere in the ruins. It was a sad thought, but perhaps that was for the best. Eustace's obsession with the girl's virginity was far beyond unseemly. Quince didn't want to think of what the vile man might have done if he had had the girl in his power.

There were footsteps approaching, scrunching and occasionally sliding on the loose sand. Quince didn't turn toward the sound, pouring some more bourbon instead.

Arnold walked into view. He stood staring into the darkness up the valley for a while before taking out one of his signature slim cigarettes and lighting it. "Good evening, Herr Professor." he said, glancing back between drags.

"Mister Arnold." Quince tossed back the whiskey and winced. He reached for the bottle.

"You are not at the dig? Surely it is a momentous event which you should attend."

"That is not archaeology!" Quince fumed, "It is plunder and sacrilege. We shall never know the truth of the temple's original use now."

"Herr Eustace is certain he knows exactly what the temple was for."

"That chinless buffoon knows nothing. Weather control, he says! What tosh! And the stupid horrible politics you people believe in."

Arnold turned to face Quince. The light from the dig cast shadows on his cheeks and made his expression hard to read. "You do not believe in the tenets of National Socialism?"

If he were sober Quince might have thought it best not to insult Nazi ideology, but he would probably have gone ahead and done it anyway. He was drunk, so the brief awareness didn't even register. "Your beliefs are vile. Let me tell you about my brother-in-law."

"Your brother-in-law? My briefing told me nothing about your family. Yes, please do tell me about your brother-in-law."

"My sister married a German Jew. There was somewhat of a controversy, we are not perfect and there is still anti-Semitism in England. I was no better than most, until I met Werner. He is one of the finest men I have ever known, and he helped me and my career incredibly. Werner is an entomologist, see, and his expertise helped me to pin down the origin of a number of mummies by identifying the bugs in their bindings. Werner lives in England now, but he has family in Germany. I know what you people are doing."

"Yes. I know what we people are doing as well, and perhaps it is wrong. But I am just.... Well, I am not just a simple soldier."

"A simple spy?"

As Arnold dragged on his cigarette, the glowing tip illuminated what might have been a thin smile. "A simple spy? Yes, I like that. I serve my country, and I have done so- and done so well- for some time. I do not appreciate all that is being done in the name of a greater Germany, but I cannot abandon it either."

"That sounds weak to me. Help stop them. Save your country."

"Perhaps I shall, but this silly little desert mystery is not worth the risk. Perhaps at a later date. I am very sorry about your assistant and all the others. I shall try to see that no more people are harmed, but I cannot make you any promises." Arnold studied his cigarette, judging whether there was another drag left in it. Disappointed, he tossed the stub away. "Goodnight, Herr Professor."

As Arnold walked, and occasionally slid, away down the slope, Quince poured himself some more whiskey.

Part 3

The tent was a solitary bright spot in the deep darkness of a desert night. There was to be a party and a show, and all the lamps had been lit so every detail could be seen.

Most of the camp was crowded into the huge marquee, sat on cushions around small, low tables. The crowd was arrayed such that there was a semicircle of free floor by the rear door flap. Through this slit in the fabric the performers would appear, for a floor show arranged by Yusuf, son of the caravan leader.

Mustafa was sat on a higher set of cushions to one side of the main door, casting the occasional proud glance at his son, who had stopped bustling around and taken a spot near the stage. The young man, it appeared, wanted to be part of the performance. This made Mustafa particularly happy- it was time the youngster started to enjoy the pleasures of the flesh.

Sat beside Mustafa were his honoured guests, the American archaeologist Montana Smith and Veronica Jiggleswick, Jiggles to her friends- the brave and beautiful English pilot who had flown Smith up the valley to this impromptu rendezvous. Miss Jiggleswick's aeroplane was near the huge lake at the head of the valley, by which she had been forced to make an emergency landing after someone had tampered with its fuel. Whilst recovering the plane, Mustafa's men had found a filled in shaft which led down to a room or tunnels. They would investigate this in the morning, but for now they were settling back to enjoy wine, food and fine exotic dancing from some of the caravan's passengers. Mustafa's main cargo was precious stones from mines far inland, and his caravan was so heavily protected that it offered safe passage to young women, and occasionally men, wishing to travel to the coast, most often to make their fortunes in the pleasure houses that thrived there. On this journey Mustafa played host to five young ladies, and Yusuf had negotiated with them to put on the show which was to follow.

A head popped through a gap in the back wall of the tent. The gorgeous dark face, with pitch black hair pulled harshly back, showed, just for a moment, surprise and nervousness at the size of the audience. The tent went quiet, and stayed quiet even after the pretty face disappeared again. As if this had been a signal, the lamps on the tables were doused, leaving the performance area lit.

There was no band, but two men with tin whistles had been press-ganged into providing a sibilant accompaniment. They started playing, but not necessarily the same tune. As a rhythm of cups on tables was taken up, then agreed, the whistles settled into the same tune.

The rear curtain split, and one of the girls shimmied out. She wasn't the one who had peeped out before. Her dark skin was even more lustrous, made shiny with oil. A silver chain looped around her waist and then around the curve of her belly, where it held up a thin strip of white material which draped down below the level of her knees, but only just covered her sex at the top. Another chain passed over the top of her chest and under her armpits, holding up two narrower, shorter strips which fluttered over the rise of her breasts and balanced on her nipples. She took a bow, and the strips of fabric billowed out in front of her. The audience members at the edges of the impromptu stage got a wonderful view which drew appreciative murmurs.

The girl stepped aside and waved at the curtain. The rest of the girls came through together. Three of them were dressed the same as the first, but in different colours- deep blue, yellow and red. The last of the girls was wearing all the material the other four had forgotten. A gauzy veil covered her face, and more scraps covered the rest of her body. They looked like they would pull off with the lightest of tugs. The four with the ribbons on flanked their demure companion, who started gyrating to the music. She raised her hands over her head as she rotated, shimmying and letting her buttocks fill out the material which covered them, teasing and tantalising with their roundness.

The veiled girl's dance revealed the shape of her body where it pushed against the material. She had full, up-tilted breasts, a narrow waist and firm, rounded buttocks. About the only secrets her costume didn't let slip were the lips of her sex and her face below her eyes. But those eyes spoke volumes in themselves. Large and dark, they shone with lust. When she had finished her gyrations they came to rest on Yusuf and didn't leave him as she began shaking her hips side to side. The girl with the blue strips leaned in close to air kiss a veiled cheek. As she pulled away she took a section of material from the veiled girl's shoulder with her.

The yellow stripped girl repeated the kiss and tug from the other side, and the veiled girl's shoulders were bare. Yusuf shuffled uncomfortably as the girl's eyebrows raised suggestively and her eyes hinted there was a smile behind the veil. She turned from him and rotated her buttock cheeks at him.

While the blue and yellow stripped girls tugged at the material covering the veiled girl's behind, white and red approached Yusuf. They offered him a hand each to help him up, then let him steady himself by resting his hands on their naked derrières. He squeezed them tight as he watched the material tear and expose the perfect moons of the veiled girl's of butt cheeks. With his eyes on the prize, the girls started to undress him.

The girls in blue and yellow went down on their knees to remove the material from the veiled girl's legs. They were getting into their roles, running their fingers over the naked skin of the revealed limbs, kissing the tops of the swaying thighs and, just maybe, sneaking up to tease at the hot pussy lips still hidden from view. The way the veiled girl's shimmy became a grind certainly suggested this was happening.

Meanwhile, red and white had stripped Yusuf naked, an achievement which had passed almost unnoticed as everyone concentrated on the dance of several veils. White turned Yusuf to face her where she knelt in front of him, allowing most of the crowd to see his attractive, gently curving erection. Red reached between his legs and gently cupped his balls as white flexed a long, almost prehensile, tongue out to lick from base to tip. Yusuf groaned, and reddened slightly when his father applauded the performance. Reluctantly, red and white turned him to face the veiled girl once more.

The veiled girl turned to face Yusuf and, as she rotated, the girls either side of her unfurled the material which covered her breasts. They held the strip of fabric between them at just the right height to shield her chest from view. At the urging of white and red, Yusuf slowly walked toward the partially hidden girl. When he was close enough, yellow and blue dropped the material and let him behold the treasures it had hidden. His hands went straight to them, cupping them and then flicking the taut nipples with his thumbs. He looked quite surprised at his own actions, then guilty. Looking into the girl's eyes he got a little nod in return, then they both glanced down. Her hips angled forward so that the light fabric which hid her sex was pushed against the tip of his penis. He flinched in surprised pleasure.

The girl nodded toward the material which hung between her legs, obviously suggesting that Yusuf should remove it. He was more than happy to do this, but first he reached up and gently tugged the veil from her face. The reveal- of a pretty face with a pert nose and wide, lustful grin- drew a gasp from the crowd. They had all, but for Jiggles and Montana, seen her before as one of the caravan's passengers, but the context left them surprised.

"Her name is Lalya." Mustafa confided in a whisper to Jiggles and Montana. "She is from a good family and is travelling to study, rather than for the reasons the other girls are making the journey." He sat back in his seat and pondered the development.

Yusuf and Lalya were staring into each other's eyes. The crowd was enraptured, waiting for the next move. When Yusuf and Lalya kissed there was applause. They didn't notice.

The girls in the strip outfits had left Lalya and Yusuf to their business and gone back out of the flap. They returned, carrying a low, padded couch between them. They put it down in the middle of the performance area and the girl in white went to Lalya and whispered in her ear.

Lalya broke the kiss and stepped back from Yusuf. She took his hands and made him clasp the one last piece of material she wore- the strip which hung between her legs. As she slowly walked backwards the material drew taut, then began slipping from the chain around her waist which held it up. Finally it pulled out completely and fluttered to the floor as Yusuf released it. Everyone, not least Yusuf himself, stared at Lalya's neatly trimmed pubic hair and the wrinkled lips below it.

Lalya sat on the couch, then lay back. With her legs spread she planted her feet flat on the floor, opening herself wide for all to see. Yusuf knelt before her and appeared to be praying, offering up praise for the beautiful sight. He rested his fingers on the insides of Lalya's thighs, moving them gently in circles. She liked that, reaching back over her head to grasp the padding as she moaned quietly.

Yusuf kissed the darkening folds of Lalya's labia, licking them and sliding his tongue between them. She cried out at this. It was, as many in the room suspected, the first time anyone had kissed her so intimately and it felt just as good as she had hoped. Her grip on the bench tightened and her feet lifted off the floor as her thighs tensed.

As Yusuf kissed and licked and probed with his tongue, and Lalya squirmed and sighed under his ministrations, the other four girls found cushions and sat on the floor to watch. Occasionally, one of them would lean in to offer the novice boy or girl some advice. Acting upon one piece of advice, Yusuf sat up, pulling his mouth away from a pussy made juicy from saliva and excitement. Lalya's whimper of disappointment was cut short as he slid two fingers into her.

Yusuf thrust his fingers in and out slowly, occasionally twisting them to change the sensations Lalya experienced. Her feet were back on the floor and, with them pushing up and her back arching, her full, firm, rounded buttocks lifted from the padding on the top of the couch. She was close, enticingly near, to orgasm. Everyone in the room was waiting for the release, expecting a sympathetic catharsis of their own when it came. But Lalya wanted something more before she climaxed. She said something to Yusuf- it was obviously an order, but it was delivered with tenderness and passion behind it.

Rising to a crouch, Yusuf brought his erection close to Lalya's hot and waiting vagina. He aimed it carefully with one hand, whilst holding her as best he could around the waist with the other. With care, and an aim that belied his passion, Yusuf guided himself into Lalya. He pushed at the slick labia, the dark head of his magnificent penis sliding through on lubrication provided by his own tongue. The head popped in easily, and they both made happy sounds.

Before he started thrusting, Yusuf grasped Lalya with both hands- each one cupping a magnificent hemisphere of buttock. Remembering that he was putting on a show, and no doubt for the pleasure of his partner as well, he took his sweet time sliding all the way into her. The whole tent hung on the tense, teasing thrust, holding their breath until he was as deep inside her as he could get. The collective sigh was matched by Lalya's moan of pure pleasure.

Yusuf started shallow movements in and out of Lalya, and she grasped him around the shoulders to hold him close. Most of the tent could see in intimate detail the way Lalya's lips clung to Yusuf's shaft as it pulled out of her. They were too intent on that to see that the other four girls were up and prowling through the crowd.

The girl with the white strips, and the one with red, were heading towards Jiggles, whilst blue and yellow approached Montana. Neither of the intended victims noticed until the girls were right in front of them.

Confused by the nearly naked women offering them helping hands out of their seats, Jiggles and Montana looked first at each other then to their host. Mustafa feigned his own confusion, but the uncontrollable smirk pointed out the lie of that. He shrugged and waved at the barely concealed beauties before his guests, suggesting that the offer be accepted. They were on their feet almost immediately.

Some of the spectators turned to watch Jiggles and Montana being led to the stage, but most were engrossed by the scene being played out by Yusuf and Lalya. The caravan's guests were flanking the floor show before most of the crowd noticed them.

Jiggles was aware of the stares she was drawing. Luckily, she had never been shy, and determined to make it a great show now she was part of it. The two girls circled her and she kept turning to follow them, until she started to get dizzy. They danced around her, examining her clothes and occasionally nipping open buttons. Before she had really registered, her blouse was completely opened and the bow on her trousers was loose so that they barely clung to her hips.

The girl in the white strips paused in front of Jiggles. She hooked her fingers inside Jiggles' blouse and pulled it open, folding back the flaps until they revealed full, firm breasts. Jiggles had chosen to do without her brassiere and the naked mammaries with tipped up and perky nipples drew an appreciative comment from the girl in white. The girl pushed the blouse off Jiggles' shoulders and ran her fingers around her areolae. Jiggles reached up and tugged at the two strips of material that covered the girl's equally magnificent breasts. The material tautened, then pulled free from the chain which held it.

Jiggles let the two strips of material flutter down from her hands, then shrugged properly out of her blouse so that it hung down from where it was tucked into the back of her trousers. They stepped together so that their breasts touched and sent tingles back and forth. Jiggles grasped the girl's waist whilst she took hold of Jiggles' trousers and pushed them down. Jiggles found the chain which held up the strip of white material and traced it to the hook which kept it together. In a moment, the girl was no longer in white, whilst Jiggles was naked from the knees up. They paused to look down and investigate each other's pubic hair. Jiggles' was dark blonde and profuse, whilst the girl's was pitch black and neatly trimmed.

Fingers lightly traced down Jiggles' spine, then tickled at the cleft at the top of her buttocks. She had completely forgotten about Red. When she looked around she found that the girl had pulled over a long couch just like the one Yusuf and Lalya were on. Remembering the young lovers, Jiggles checked them out as she sat down. They were lovingly coupled on their couch, Lalya with her legs back against her chest and hooked over Yusuf's shoulders, letting him thrust as deeply as possible into her. The flush of their skin, and their expressions, said they were close to climax.

Beyond Yusuf and Lalya, Montana was getting similar treatment to Jiggles. He had been stripped of his clothes and now stood poised- magnificent erection held by one of the girls- ready to sit on a couch of his own. When he had lowered himself, the girl who had held his member scooted around to kneel before him. Gently cupping his balls and holding his hard on at the base, she started licking along its length, twirling her tongue around the tip before licking back down it. Montana lay back to smile up at the other girl who tended him- the only one who still wore any clothing, the blue strip hanging down before her crotch. She flipped the material over Montana's face so that he was the only one who could see her pubis, then moved to crouch so that he could kiss it.

Jiggles brought her attention back to her own situation. She sat on the couch and lifted her legs so that white could pull her shoes and trousers off. The girl hooked Jiggles' legs over her shoulders and lowered her mouth to the inviting, crinkled lips of her pussy. Smiling up at the girl who had been in red, white signalled with her eyes that she should straddle Jiggles' head the way Montana's head was being straddled.

As Red's crotch filled Jiggles' vision and white's tongue played with her pussy lips and occasionally flicked at her clitoris, the rest of the tent went away. The plump lips were full, smooth and warm, and glistened with excitement as they moved closer to Jiggles' mouth. Jiggles sneaked her tongue out and thrust it between the lips. The girl sitting on her face gave an appreciative gasp. She flinched away for a moment, then lowered herself for more of the pleasure Jiggles' tongue offered.

The girl between Jiggles' thighs had hit a rhythm, her tongue pushing between the wrinkled lips and then pushing up until the flat of it pressed against the nub of the clitoris, and rotating before heading back down. Jiggles tried to match the rhythm, albeit working from the top to the bottom of the slit bearing down on her. Even with firm, slightly quivering calves clasped either side of her head Jiggles could still hear the cries of Lalya and Yusuf as they reached a near simultaneous climax. With her lips pressed against a hot, slick pussy, Jiggles couldn't make as much noise, but her groans resonated through the pelvis of the girl who rode her face.

Jiggles felt that she was floating away from the couch, particularly when a pair of fingers slid into her, augmenting the tongue that now swirled around her clitoris. The pleasure she expressed was transmitted to the girl riding her face, who did a good job of voicing it. As she came, Jiggles nearly threw both of the girls off her. They held on tight, crying out climaxes of their own, then slowly slid to the floor.

The tent was silent, but for contented sighs. Then the crowd began applauding, loudly and enthusiastically. Jiggles looked around, still dazed, and slowly remembered where she was. She waved acknowledgement to her fans then relaxed back onto the couch. "I think I shall just sleep here tonight." she announced.

* * *

Fiona was roused by kisses from Kita, and aroused by the gentle flicking of the girl's fingers on her nipples. As her eyes struggled open she was greeted by a smile almost as bright as the morning light outside their cave. Kita spoke quickly and excitedly, forgetting that Fiona only understood one word in every five. Kita was going to find some breakfast, perhaps Fiona would like to stay here and wake Ally. They both looked down at the lovely naked girl beside them. Fiona had to agree, it was a good idea.

Kita stood and walked, naked, from the cave. Casually as anything, she greeted a passer-by as the curtain closed. Fiona had savoured the view of the girl's rolling buttocks as she crossed the floor, but now she turned her attention to the beauty beside her. Using a proven technique, she kissed Ally and played with her nipples. As Ally responded, Fiona's fingers started travelling down her body, tickling the sensitive smooth skin.

Ally squirmed over onto her back and stretched and spread her legs. Fiona ran her fingers through Ally's springy pubic hair, enjoying the way it pushed back. Below the hair, the nub of Ally's clitoris tempted Fiona's fingers. She nipped the fleshy sheath which shielded the nub and Ally wriggled under the pressure. She wanted to escape the intense pleasure at the same time as desiring more of it.

Fiona began moving her fingertips in circles on Ally's clitoris, swirling in wider and faster arcs as she got into the rhythm. They both moved, so that Fiona could lock her lips to one of Ally's breasts and slide two fingers into her now slick vagina. As Ally's left leg lifted, Fiona clasped it between her thighs and rubbed against it. Having teased the nipple up to a peak, Fiona moved to the other breast.

Ally writhed with pleasure, almost throwing Fiona off as her fingers pumped in and out. Inspired, Fiona rolled with Ally's movements, ending up on the floor on her back with the brunette atop her. Fiona's fingers were still inside Ally, but the back of her hand was pressed down against her own crotch. As Ally rode Fiona's fingers she was grinding the girl's knuckles against her sensitive mons and clitoris, paying back the pleasure. Fiona's free hand came up to clasp a perfect, hemispherical breast and support Ally as she climaxed.

Resting on Fiona's chest, Ally kissed her shoulders and neck as she gyrated against the fingers still in her. As Ally ground herself to another orgasm, Fiona's own climax neared. They kissed, tongues playing against each other as they came together.

Ally slid off Fiona and they lay together, grinning. "Good morning." Fiona said with a happy lilt.

* * *

Ginge awoke to the delicious feeling of a pair of tongues flicking and teasing at his growing hard on. Uncertain where he was, his inner ear told him he was floating, swaying in an irregular arc. Distracted by the licking and teasing, it took him some time to remember he was on a hammock in a cave in the desert.

The story of how Ginge came to be in the cave- with the archaeologist Amid and Amid's step-cousin Sorya- was convoluted and confusing. Amid and Ginge had run away from an archaeological dig site in the desert, fleeing Nazi raiders, and found their way to Sorya's eyrie. She and Amid were sworn to guard the secrets of the temple Amid was helping to dig up, and the Nazis were trying to steal them- convinced they would endow the Fuhrer with supernatural powers. Plied with aphrodisiac tea, Ginge had let the confusion pass in favour of a ménage with Amid and his step-cousin.

It didn't matter whose lips were around the head of Ginge's cock- the cousins were equally adept in the oral arts. He hazarded opening his eyes to take a look around. Unexpectedly, he was presented with the view of a wrinkled, and tightening, ball sack and a large, throbbing penis. Amid had, ever so carefully, straddled Ginge's head and was now working his lips down the throbbing shaft of little Ginge. Sorya was kneeling before the hammock and nibbling at Ginge's testicles with her lips.

Amid moved slightly, and the straining head of his cock hovered over Ginge's lips. Ginge clasped it, gently but firmly, and sucked at it. He could just get the head of Amid's erection into his mouth, their positions would allow no more, but his tongue attacked it with gusto. Amid hardly broke the rhythm of his sucking, but his hips began a gentle gyration which rotated the crown of his member in Ginge's mouth.

Sorya sat back and watched, her fingers playing around and into her engorged pussy lips. Her cousin and his lover were close to climax, they would not need any more help from her. Her free hand played with her breasts, teasing and tweaking the nipples.

The hammock swung in an odd pattern, driven by the movements of Amid and Ginge. As they grew more excited, and their heads bobbed faster, it settled into a more regular back and forth sway. Sensing imminent orgasm, Amid sucked less of Ginge's engorged tool with each bob of his head. He felt the twitch as semen was pumped up Ginge's shaft. Sticky, warm liquid hit the tip of his tongue, then the back of it as Ginge's second spurt was stronger. He swallowed it, sucking hungrily even as Ginge paused in his own ministrations to moan.

It was mere moments before Ginge renewed his licking and sucking of the head of Amid's now quivering hard on, and not much longer before his actions had the desired effect. As Amid climaxed, Ginge pressed the flat of his tongue over the head of the cock in his mouth, as if to hold the spurting spunk in.

Eventually, the hammock stopped swinging and Amid rolled aside from straddling Ginge's head. There was a cry from the floor and they both looked down to see Sorya bringing herself to climax, the flat of her hand moving rapidly over her mons.

When they had all come down from the bliss of their orgasms, Sorya was the first to start dressing. "We shall go to the camp where the rest of the priestesses are." she announced. "You shall be reacquainted with your friends, Ginge, and we can plan our next actions."

* * *

Jiggles awoke under fluttering gauze and it felt like one of her dreams of flying. Warm, naked flesh rubbed against her, even in the cold desert night she had needed no cover. Either side of her were the women she had made love with the night before. To her left, Montana was wrapped in his lovers, one of them already caressing his fattening penis.

Everyone was waking, memories of the night before arousing them from their slumber. There might have been a pleasurable repeat, with some new combinations, of the previous night's action, if their host had not breezed into the tent. "Good morning. Good morning. Good morning." Mustafa hailed, "Ladies and honoured guests we shall have a light repast and then our mystery well is ready to be explored."

Montana rubbed his eyes and struggled into a near sitting position. "I'm sorry, have we slept late?"

"Not at all. I am.... enthusiastic this morning. My son has just found his future wife and I am about to investigate a possible treasure trove. I apologise, but I am somewhat excited."

Whilst Mustafa had been talking, expressing himself animatedly and walking back and forth, large metal pots of tea and bowls of surprisingly fresh fruit had been brought into the tent and laid on small tables. Montana shrugged and rose, walking over to a table and sitting cross-legged before it. Jiggles decided to follow suit and, one by one, the women joined them.

Ravenous from their exertions of the night before and at ease in their bodies, they sat in the nude, eating and drinking as many members of the caravan's company bustled in and out. When the food was cleared away, there were clean clothes ready for them all. They dressed quickly and joined Mustafa and his son Yusuf- wrapped around his bride to be- who were ready with their fine horses for the ride out to the mysterious hole they had discovered the day before.

When Jiggles and Montana had last seen the construction it had been full of sand and rocks. These had been cleared out now, revealing what could be a small cellar with a door almost as large as the wall it was in. Through the door was darkness, the light that did enter illuminated a few unmoved stones and little else. A ladder led down into the chamber and lamps, torches and tools had been left on the floor.

Mustafa leant over the edge of the cellar and looked down. "After you, Mister Montana, Miss Jiggles." he offered. Montana didn't hesitate before hopping onto the ladder and sliding down it. Jiggles made her way down much more carefully, stepping from rung to rung and consciously rolling her buttocks for him to watch. Stepping off at the bottom, she was disappointed to find Montana was already through the door and investigating the mysterious room beyond. She sighed, picked up a torch of her own, lit it and followed him.

The room was just over twice the width of the antechamber, with a low ceiling. Every three or four paces, there was a step, and every third step a pair of square pillars. The chamber descended into the distance, further than Montana's or Jiggles' torches could throw their light. "What do you think this is?" Jiggles asked.

Montana played the light from his torch across the walls, studying the stonework. "Well, it's grand in its own way, so it must be something important. But the construction, the finish, is rather rough and basic. This is not a temple, but it is something important."

Jiggles waved her torch into the darkness. "That direction, that's the lake. Do you think this goes under it?"

"I can't wait to find out."

Mustafa and Yusuf had come down the ladder, with four of the men from the caravan, who were carrying picks, shovels and large pry bars. "Shall we go?" Mustafa suggested.

* * *

Kita brought food, clothes and her gorgeous bright smile. When Ally and Fiona were dressed- in similar simple but attractive outfits to hers- she sat with them. Slowed by the act of eating, her enthusiastic explanations were easier for Fiona to follow. After clarifying a few points, she nodded and smiled, "Kita says a man with hair of copper is with her sister and cousin at the lookout."

"That sounds like Ginge. Her cousin?" Ally asked.

"Amid." Kita informed them.

"Of course." Ally picked up a piece of bread, studied it and took a bite. "Does she know anything about Jiggles and Doctor Smith?"

Kita smiled and started explaining something else to them. "Your aeroplane landed at the very head of the valley, by the great lake. The passengers were not hurt and are now with a trade caravan. They are trying to get a message to them, to tell them about the raid on the dig. We still don't know where Professor Quince is, though. And it appears that Eustace has betrayed us all and teamed up with the raiders."

Fiona asked Kita some more questions, and came back with, "There will be a rescue raid later today, or tomorrow at the latest. They would like us to sneak into the temple complex before the raid."

Ally considered this. It sounded risky, but no more so than what they had gone through the previous day. "Why?"

"I'm not sure. Kita said something about treasure, and that the head priestess will explain."

When the food had been cleared away, they were joined by the oarsmen from their boat ride the day before, the senior priestess and her translator. "We will send you first." he announced after the priestess had addressed them. "Kita knows the temple intimately and you are both resourceful ladies. Then we will send men when they arrive here."

"So it will be just us over there?" Ally asked.

"At first, but not for long. They will not have removed the rubble yet, or reached into the catacombs at all. You will be safe."

"It still seems a touch risky, for no real reason."

"Oh, I assure you, there is a reason. We have counted our treasures and it seems we have left some in the temple in our rush to evacuate after the attack. Kita knows where to find them, and you can be in and out really quick. By the time you are done, a raiding party will have crossed and you come back."

Fiona and Ally considered the plan, and nodded. "We will do it." Fiona declared, translating her message before the short man by the priestess had a chance.

Once the decision had been made, they started moving quickly. The only remnants of their clothing from the day before were sturdy, high ankled boots, ideal for walking through the dust and stones of the desert. They were an incongruous addition to the simple traditional clothes they had been gifted, but their feet were too tender for the thin slippers Kita favoured. They were offered short swords, which hung on scabbards slung over their shoulders and, thus armed, headed into the caves at the foot of the encampment.

The oarsmen led the way into the caves, stepping gently from stone to stone without needing the lamps Ally, Fiona and Kita held. They climbed into the boat- they could fit another two people in at a push, it was going to be a small raiding party that followed them. They tried not to think about the logistics as they floated across the darkness of the underground lake.

* * *

The hallway had continued down a long, long way, narrowing as it went. Very slowly, the walls had edged in until they touched the pillars, then the pillars merged with the walls and they were walking along a corridor just wide enough for two people. It was, however, now tall enough for them to stand up straight again.

Soon, their torches began to pick out details at the end of the corridor. Step by step, the carved stone door resolved out of the darkness. It had a face, leonine and savage, with tiny glittering dots of eyes, carved into it. When they were right up to the door they found that the eyes were deep red rubies set in the stonework. Mustafa studied them, looking with his hands as much as his eyes. "These are good stones." he commented, "They may have come from mines in my hills, they have the right colour to them." He looked closer, not so subtly testing to see if they would pry loose. "There are legends of ancient mines. I must go looking for them when I am home again."

"I would like to search for them with you." Montana said with a grin. "But first let's see if we can open this door. There may be treasure behind it." He studied the gap around the door and pushed at one edge and then the other. Nodding, he reached back and took a pry bar which had been offered.

Montana wedged the bar between the door and frame on its right hand side and heaved. With a grinding, scraping sound, the door started to move. Soon the gap was too wide for the metal bar, but the door was moving more easily. Yusuf and Montana put their weight behind the door and it scratched open slowly. The air inside, which flowed out and around them slowly, was cold and damp. They all shivered so much that the beams from their lamps danced around the inside of the revealed room.

When their teeth had stopped chattering and they were able to hold the torches steady, they dared to cross the threshold. Montana went first, with Jiggles right beside him. Yusuf and Mustafa followed closely behind and the four caravan crew waited at the threshold, uncertain.

The room was large, but not so grand that the corners swallowed up the light from their lamps. The walls were damp enough to glisten, but not to hide the hieroglyphs carved in them, whilst there was a thin sheen of water on the floor. Montana looked closely at the shapes cut into one wall, whilst Jiggles crouched down to study the patterns in the floor. She traced the raised outline of a large figure of some sort carved into the stonework.

"If only Fiona were here. She's so much better at these dead languages than me." Montana admitted. He began translating. "He who walks with the eagle shall.... Walks with the eagle, shall release the.... I'm not sure what this symbol is, I think it may be a god. This," he pointed out zigzag lines to Yusuf and Mustafa, who were eagerly watching his translation, "means water, I'm sure. Considering how long it is, it probably means a river. So, he who walks with the eagle shall release the god of the river."

"Where is this eagle it speaks of?" asked Mustafa.

"I think it is right here." Jiggles announced. She had stood and was wiping water away from a damp knee. She pointed at the pattern she had revealed in the floor, a wide spread, flame-like wing leading up to the head and sharp beak of a stylised bird of prey. "Could this be your eagle?"

There was a shout from the doorway, where the caravan crew were pointing at the floor. There was now a lip below the edge of the doorway which had not been there before. "The floor is sinking?" Mustafa translated incredulously. "That is ridiculous."

Montana played his torch beam around the base of the wall, spotting a paler band of stone which had been revealed in the time they had been in the room. It was only a couple of inches deep, but slowly, inexorably and- obviously now they looked closely- growing. "Oh, this cannot be good." Montana declared.

The foreboding was justified. With the tearing crack of splintering wood, the floor dropped a foot. A low wave of water washed across the stonework, knocking everyone off their feet. "Get out of here!" Montana yelled, before being hit in the face by the backwash.

The water pouring into the room pushed them toward the door, so that part was easy enough. But they struggled to stand up again and had to reach up for the grasping hands of the caravan crew. Yusuf was pulled out first. He sat on the edge of the door and helped haul his father in. As Mustafa struggled away up the corridor, Yusuf and the crew grabbed Montana and he grasped Jiggles' wrist.

Another sound broke through the roar of running water, the splintering cracking of wooden beams. With a horrendous screech, whatever held the floor up gave way and it, and gallons of water, toppled into a deep black pit. Jiggles swung over the chasm, clinging as tightly as she could to Montana's wrist. The water pouring in from the opposite side of the room hit the wall just below Jiggles' boots, and a cloud of droplets almost enveloped her. When she had stopped swaying, her feet scrabbled against the brickwork until they found purchase and she was boosted up and into Montana's embrace.

"What just happened?" Jiggles asked, shivering from the shock and cold.

Montana sat up, helping Jiggles into a sitting position. He took a torch that had been dropped and shone it into the hole. There was nothing to see but the rushing water. "I believe we have released the river god."

As they started back up the tunnel there was another roar and crashing as large sections of the wall across the hole collapsed and a greater deluge of water poured out. The air forced out of the hole rushed past them like a wind, raising dust and stinging their eyes. The floor beneath their feet shook with the power of the torrent. "We should run." Montana announced. "Fast. Let's get out of here."

* * *

Ally and Fiona still didn't know their way around the temple's corridors, but Kita gave the impression she could find her way around without the lamp she carried. Every so often she would stop to point out a detail on the wallway points or history it was never certain. Very soon, they were in a small side room and Kita was pointing at two small statues and a large leather-bound book.

Kita took the book and Ally and Fiona had a statue each. They hurried out of the room and back down the corridor. They turned left into a smaller corridor at one of Kita's way points and found themselves facing three armed men. The men didn't move, or even raise their weapons. The girls turned, to run the other way, to see three more men step out of the shadows. One of them was Eustace, and he grinned evilly.

"My, my, my. We thought you were dead Fiona. This is good, it means I have my sacrifice again."

* * *

There were three men, two priestesses and the two oarsmen in the boat, ready to cross the cave lake. It had taken them longer than planned to assemble all the equipment they needed, and they had already had a false start when they found the boat was overloaded. They had gone less than three boat lengths from the shore before deciding that the gunnels were too close to the water's surface for safety and turning back.

Now they were ready to set off again. Instructions were shouted to and from the shore, last minute decisions about what and who would come over in the next boatload and final orders. Then the oarsmen pulled away from the shore with two strong strokes and they were off.

The journey across the lake in the cave was normally a simple affair once the boat was lined up. They could not easily go off course, as piles driven into the lake bed would rub gently against the hull and signal needed corrections. This time, however, it was not so easy. There was a wind blowing across the lake, something that never happened. The boat was driven sharply off course and ground hard against one of the pilings. The planking flexed and cracked, letting a little water in.

The wind twisted the boat around the piling and pushed it completely off course. It grounded on low lying rocks and tipped over on to its side. The priestesses tumbled out and one of the oarsmen followed them. The wind was whipping up waves on the normally placid water, lapping it into the boat. The rest of the passengers and the remaining oarsman jumped out and started struggling for the lamps on the near shore.

The water was shallow, but full of rocks. They slipped and stumbled and were buffeted by the waves and the wind. Eventually, one by one, they slid off the rocks and into the deeper channel. They swam the short distance to the bank they had left and struggled ashore. Helped up by the compatriots they had left behind, they limped out of the suddenly strange and stormy cave.

* * *

They had struck camp and been waiting when Sorya's servant arrived with horses for them. "We will meet your friends at the encampment, if they have completed their little mission. Then we shall see how many men there are to help us re-take the dig site." Sorya announced.

"Mission?" Ginge queried as Sorya spurred her horse off. Amid shrugged.

They headed out of the amphitheatre the cave was in and followed the newly worn track Sorya's servant had created. Ginge had some experience with horses and found the ride this morning far more comfortable than the one the day before when they had arrived on camels. The path led down the hill on the other side and wandered as best it could toward another line of low, jagged peaks. The sun was still low enough not to sear them and, after the chaos of the previous day, it was a refreshing ride.

A little over an hour later they rounded a sharply stepped butte and were faced with a wide ravine leading down between the peaks. People bustled around in the bottom of the ravine, some with a sense of urgency bordering on panic but many more with purpose and some yet to be revealed plan. As Sorya, Ginge and Amid rode into the ravine, people stopped to watch them.

Sorya dismounted beside a senior looking priestess who had waved her over. They talked. The priestess was obviously troubled and kept gesturing down the ravine. When the conversation was over Amid and Ginge joined them.

"Something has gone wrong." Sorya announced, "My sister and Ally and Fiona are trapped in the temple. There is a cave," she waved down the ravine, "with an underground lake in it. It is our secret way into the temple. Kita and the others had crossed the lake and another party was crossing to swap with them when..... a great wind blew in and made it impossible to cross the lake."

"Wind? Underground?" Ginge was as confused now as Sorya.

"I know. They do not know where it could have risen from. We were supposed to sneak some of our relief party into the temple, for the surprise. Now we have people trapped over there."

"The river god has been released." Amid announced with awe.

Sorya gave her step-cousin a confused look. "Surely you do not suddenly believe in the gods?"

"No, not at all. But I do know the history of our cult. We guard the secrets that have been handed down, but there have always been rumours that there are secrets that even we do not know. The rivers were set up so that the Valley of the Wizards could have water running through it again. What if the water flows through the cave with our underground lake in it. I believe someone may have found the trigger to release the river into the valley."

"That sounds like the sort of thing that Jiggles would do." Ginge commented.

"There are still fifty men and priestesses ready to attack the dig and take it back before they desecrate the temple too much." Sorya announced, "It will have to be a more open attack, however, without the sneak elements we had hoped for."

"There is the tunnel Amid used to get us out of the camp." Ginge suggested.

"If they haven't found it, then maybe we could get a few people in using it." Amid conceded.

"So, what are we waiting for? Can someone get me a gun?" Ginge volunteered.

* * *

When they reached daylight again, the temple exploration team was coated in dust and mud. The wind had just stopped howling through the tunnel as the hole had finally filled, but the structure still shook from the extreme force of thousands of tons of water cascading into it. They looked like animated statues as they clambered up the ladder. But they didn't receive the reception they expected.

The rest of the crew, who had been coated with dust themselves as the gale blew back along the tunnel, were now staring at the surface of the lake. As Jiggles, Montana, Mustafa and Yusuf approached the crowd they too spotted the sight that held their attention. Some way out from the shore, the lake surface bubbled and frothed around a hole in the water. After the chaos of the tunnel it took them some time for their ears to adjust so that they could hear the roar of the water falling.

"We pulled the plug on the lake." Montana said with awe.

The nearest members of the crowd heard the comment and turned to see the apparitions that had clambered out of the hole. They cried out in shock then came over to check what they had seen. Within moments the dirt coated crew were surrounded by a loud, babbling crowd. Eventually Mustafa managed to quiet them and he and Yusuf explained what they had just experienced.

Jiggles and Montana edged out of the group and walked down to the lake's edge. The water level had noticeably dropped, with a line of still damp mud showing where it had previously been. "All that water must be going somewhere." Jiggles noted.

"Maybe it comes out somewhere in the Valley of the Wizards. Or perhaps it's all underground. If we can get your plane in the air maybe we can track it."

The sound of the crowd had changed again. Jiggles and Montana turned to find out what was happening now. Everyone was watching a pair of riders galloping from the direction of the caravan's encampment. The horses wheeled to a halt in front of the crowd and the jockeys leapt off. Unable to recognise Mustafa they were initially confused, until the crowd parted to reveal him. After double takes at his state, the newcomers started telling a tale which was obviously grand and important.

Montana and Jiggles found Yusuf. "What are they saying?" Montana asked.

"Your dig site was attacked, and they blew up the temple, or damaged it, anyway. The priestesses are planning an attack to take it back." Yusuf stopped for a moment, listening to a new development. He nodded, "They say that your friends are alive and well, and working with them. If your aeroplane is flying, they wonder if you might help as well."

"Yes." Jiggles answered without a second thought.

"Well I guess so." Montana agreed.

Mustafa turned to Jiggles and Montana, "I take it my son has translated for you?"

"Yes." Jiggles and Montana answered in unison.

"And you will help?" There were nods as replies. "Very good. I have men who will come with you."

"And I will go as well." Yusuf offered.

"Of course. We only have hunting rifles. Powerful, but not very rapid fire. We also have dynamite, can you drop it from your airplane?"

"We can take the windows out and the door off, if we don't fly too high. It gets awfully cold at altitude." Jiggles started walking toward her Hawker "Hooligan"- still parked near the lake shore where they had left it the night before- as she pondered the technicalities out loud. The crowd started following her. "We can seat four down the door side and five on the other, with one person in the door to drop the dynamite." Jiggles stopped by her plane. "You fixed the wheel." she noted, "That is good work."

"How soon can you take off?" Mustafa asked.

"How soon can you get the men and guns here?"

The Hooligan had been forced down by a blockage in the fuel line. Whilst the men and weapons were rounded up Jiggles investigated the cause of the blockage. As she had suspected, there was water in the secondary fuel tank. With Montana's help, she unblocked the line and emptied the tank. With a little bit of work, they separated the water out of the fuel mix and poured it back in. "We should have just about enough juice to get us back to the dig site and do a few circuits before we run out." she confided to Montana and Yusuf, "I hope that is enough to get the job done."

With the gunners and bombardier on board and the windows and door piled up safely they were ready for take off. "We shall bring you those parts." Mustafa reassured Jiggles before stepping down from the plane, "I would like to see this dig of yours." He embraced his son and then hurried away to a safe vantage point.

The engines started first time, then spluttered and faltered. Jiggles throttled up, and the whole airframe shook as the engines spat and coughed the last of the water out of the system. She looked back at her passengers. Tough men, all of them, they were trying to hide their fear. None of them but for Yusuf had been in the air before, and they were beginning to regret the bravado which had made them volunteer for this adventure.

As the Hooligan began to roll forward, Jiggles steered it to find the perfect line down the rough airstrip that had been scraped out of the desert. Tall poles marked out the location of the hole they had been down earlier. When Jiggles had made an emergency landing the day before, the plane had missed the stonework by mere feet. This time she aimed wide of it.

They gained speed as the aeroplane bounced and vibrated across the dirt. The horizon became a blur before the tailplane lifted. They were getting faster, but still the plane did not lift off. "Get ready to pull back on your stick when I tell you." Jiggles told Montana. He grasped the yoke which was wriggling in front of him.

"We don't seem to have much......" Montana decided not to finish his observation.

"Pull back, now!" Jiggles called out. Montana did as ordered. For a moment, nothing happened. Then, abruptly, the shaking stopped and he felt himself pressed down into the co-pilot's seat. They were in the air. "It's okay, I've got it now." Jiggles announced, "Easy." They started banking as they climbed, and headed for the Valley of the Wizards.

* * *

Eustace brandished Fiona's sword. "Yes, this shall be far better for the sacrifice than the blade I was going to use. This one is more..... genuine." He sheathed the sword and hung the scabbard over his shoulder. "Now, move. I have to get back to the temple chamber and see how they are getting on."

"No." Fiona stood her ground. "Not without Ally and Kita"

"Oh, that's her name is it?" Eustace eyed Kita up and down, but didn't really see past the colour of her skin. She and Ally were, in Eustace's words, to "stay behind". The implication for their longer term survival was obvious. "If it will make you complain less."

"You plan to kill me?" Fiona asked after Ally and Kita had joined her. She sounded remarkably calm given what she was talking about.

Eustace had started walking away, confident, now, that they would follow him. "A sacrifice, to tap into the powers of the valley. We can use them properly, better than they have been used."

"You know that is nonsense, don't you? The temple is not for sacrifice, it never was. It's a sex cult."

"Oh, I'm sure it degenerated into that. But everyone knows that true power comes from death. I need a virgin with royal lineage to sacrifice. Unfortunately for you my dear, that virgin is you." Eustace stopped and turned on his heel, angry at a sudden thought. "You are still a virgin, aren't you? This slut hasn't corrupted you, has she?" he pointed at Ally.

Fiona slapped Eustace, hard enough to raise a red hand print on his cheek. For a moment, it looked like he was going to hit her back, but he controlled himself. "You'll do. You'll get a fitting end."

As Eustace turned away, a gust of frigid wind blew up the corridor, rustling clothing and sending a chill through everyone. It did not feel the sort of wind which could bode well.

* * *

Ginge crawled to the top of the dusty rise and stared across at the dig site. All of the raiders, at least, all the ones he could see, were crowded around the main hole of the site. Amid joined him, and set to counting the raiders. "There were many more than that yesterday. Where have they gone." he pondered.

"Into the hole?" Ginge suggested.

"I suppose. It will make our task easier." Amid signalled to the ten men who had come with them and they followed him and Ginge back down the slope and, crouching, along the gully. They were heading away from the dig, but met a branching gully which headed back. This one zigged and zagged somewhat, but they were soon at a familiar section. Amid and Ginge scrambled up the scree to find the hidden board which covered the hole they had come out of the previous day.

They gently lifted the cover aside, raising as little dust as possible, and let it slide down the slope. The tunnel which was revealed was just a crawl space, but it made its way under the camp's walk ways and would let them sneak into the heart of the camp. Pushing a satchel full of ammunition in first, Amid slithered lithely through the gap with pistol in hand. Ginge had been issued with a rifle, which he unslung from his back and pushed before him. His entry to the tunnel was far clumsier than Amid's, and he was constantly in danger of jamming his gun between the walls as he moved, but he was moving quickly soon enough and felt no trace of the claustrophobia he had experienced the previous time he had crawled through here.

Five of the men in the squad followed Amid and Ginge into the tunnel. The other five clambered to the top of the gully to provide covering fire. The attack, when it came, would be from a different quadrant, so these marksmen would sow confusion and give the impression of a far larger force.

When Ginge had last been in the tunnels below the dig site he had been dazed and confused. The site had just come under attack and he had been shot at by Eustace. He still wasn't sure what the chinless wonder was playing at, but it appeared to involve siding with the Germans. Ginge didn't follow the news closely- unless it pertained to aeronautics or sexual scandal- but he had heard only bad things about the Nazi party. Coupled with the tales his father had told of the Hun and his battles with them in the Great War, this led to Ginge being suspicious of anyone of a Prussian nature.

They came to a junction. Here the spur of the tunnel they were in met with another which was hidden below the wooden walkways constructed to ease the flow of wheelbarrows full of rubble and sandy soil. Some of the original dig crew had to have created these for Amid and his allies, to allow them to sneak in and out of the camp and remove any sacred relics deemed too revealing for European or American eyes. It was easy to forget, when a common enemy presented itself, that Amid had been working to keep some of the secrets of the Valley of the Wizards away from outsiders. Ginge pondered this for a moment, then decided to forget it again.

Amid signalled to stop, and Ginge passed the message back along the column. Shuffling around until he was on his back, Amid moved aside a plank in the tunnel's ceiling. Leading with his pistol, he poked head, shoulders and arm through the gap. Finding no immediate danger, he climbed out, removed a couple more planks and then reached in for his ammunition pouch.

Ginge's exit from the tunnel was as graceless as his entry. Even with Amid taking his rifle and helping him up it was still a clumsy and dusty performance. Amid pointed to a stack of barrels and they crouch-ran to them. The rest of the squad came out of the tunnels and joined them, the last man replacing the planking.

They were slightly down slope from the main office tent of the dig. The radio tent- which had been tacked onto the side of the marquee, and which Amid had sliced open when they made their escape- had been pulled down and was now a pile of canvas and equipment. The flap door which had led from the larger tent to the smaller one was half open but unguarded. Leaving two of his men by the barrels to provide cover, Amid led Ginge and the rest to the tent.

The radio equipment- shattered and sabotaged by Eustace before his co-conspirators' attack- provided some cover outside the tent. Here, Amid gave instructions using hand signals before they carried on. Amid, Ginge and one of the men headed for the flap doorway, whilst the other two would flank either side of the tent.

Standing outside the door, they could hear voices. Professor Quince- the rotund, somewhat arrogant archaeologist Jiggleswick Air had brought from

England- was pleading with someone. "You have to stop the idiot. There is no magical power here, you know that. And human sacrifice is simply barbaric." there was a pause and a sigh, "Oh what use is it talking of barbarism to a Nazi thug like you."

The voice that replied did so in precise English, with obvious intonation on the German word he used, "It pains me, Herr Professor, but your former assistant effectively outranks me. I can do nothing to halt his folly. He would simply laugh at me. Or have me shot."

Through the flap, Amid and Ginge could just make out three figures. The Professor was sitting down beside one of the long work tables, addressing a tall thin man who paced back and forth as he spoke. Watching them, with his back to the door, was a guard with a machine pistol. Ginge held up his rifle and made a motion with it, striking air with the butt. Amid nodded understanding.

Ginge stepped through the flap, coming up behind the guard with his rifle raised. He cracked the butt hard against the unsuspecting man's head. The guard didn't go down immediately. Rather, he swayed on his feet, unsteady but still upright. Ginge was about to clock him again when he collapsed sideways. The man who was with Amid and Ginge caught the guard before he hit the floor and quietly laid him down and disarmed him.

Whilst the guard was being disabled, Amid had stepped around him and pointed his pistol at the tall man. "Do not make a sound." he suggested. The thin man raised his hands and nodded.

There was a scuffle at the front of the tent and the two men who had gone around the sides entered with the limp body of another guard. Quince, who had been staring open mouthed at the unexpected rescue, finally managed to speak, "My goodness! You must hurry, that damnable fool Eustace thinks he must sacrifice poor Fiona to unlock the valley's secrets. You have to rescue her!"

*** ***

The gale which had been screeching around the cave abruptly halted. The water that had been pushing the air before it arrived with a rumbling boom, flooding into the cavern through an opening somewhere in the darkness.

The lake tried to swallow the water but still a wave washed across from one end to the other.

The wave lifted the boat off the rocks and pushed it against the cavern wall. As the water level rose, the boat scraped along the cave walls, pushed along by new currents. For long moments it pirouetted above the submerged hole some- but not enough- of the water was draining through. Then it moved on again, bobbing on open water until it found itself caught in a familiar channel, heading for a beach it knew well. Inch by inch it was pushed up the slope by the rising waters until it wedged in the doorway to the temple's tunnels. Slowly, it ground its way through the gap.

* * *

The Hooligan flew low over a phalanx of horsemen and camel riders. They wheeled and stared up at the flying machine, but didn't raise their guns. "I do believe we have found the cavalry." Montana commented. "Maybe we should land and talk to them."

Jiggles studied the ground as they circled. "Not here. We would be splinters in no time. I can put some flaps on and throttle back so that we don't arrive too far ahead of them."

"Then they will have longer to react to hearing us coming!" Yusuf shouted over the wind and engine noise. He had fashioned a harness to keep himself inside the plane, even as he leant out to throw dynamite. He had been checking the sticks, and the fuses in them, for the whole flight. Now he was looking at the trench lighter hung around his neck, flicking the knurled striking wheel and testing the flame in the wind.

"You're just itching for a fight, aren't you?" Montana suggested. He turned to Jiggles, "Maybe we should soften them up and then get clear."

"Okay." Jiggles stopped circling and turned toward the dig site.

They were flying low, to stay out of sight for as long as possible, but in this vast empty space they would still be heard long before they arrived. "We should see them just as we clear that ridge." Montana pointed. He turned to the rear cabin and used gestures to repeat the message. The gunners settled in to their fighting positions.

They cleared the ridge so low that they raised dust. As the ground dropped away again they scoped out targets. Figures were running around the main hole, but something else caught Montana's attention. "Those vehicles aren't ours. What say we take them out?" Jiggles adjusted direction. "Okay Yusuf, we've found something for you to drop those sticks on!"

Some of the agitated figures stopped and pointed toward the Hooligan. Then they started running some more. The plane was almost on top of them before any of them thought to pick up a gun and fire at it. There was a crack as one of the bullets tore through the wing. It was the only of the first volley which hit the Hooligan. The loud reports of the rifles in the rear of the cabin drowned out the engine noise.

Some of the troops hit the ground as the plane passed over them, but it was impossible to tell whether they had been shot or were just diving for cover. Yusuf held three of the sticks of dynamite and had lit all of the fuses. As they passed close to the line of vehicles, he tossed them and grabbed some more. One of the sticks bounced wide, another skidded under a vehicle and the third landed in a truck bed amongst petrol cans. Men in and around the vehicles scattered.

As the plane banked, allowing the riflemen clear shots at the running figures, the dynamite exploded one after another. The petrol ignited, and a tall yellow flame blossomed from the truck bed, before folding over itself and turning orange. A shock-wave of heat shook the Hooligan as it came around for a second pass over the vehicles..

More of the soldiers on the ground were firing on the plane now, and their aim was improving. There were holes in the fuselage now, and one of the gunners had fallen back from his window, bleeding.

Yusuf threw another three sticks of dynamite as they passed over the trucks. They took more hits, and one of the engines was beginning to sound unhappy. "Time to go." Jiggles throttled up and pointed the plane away from the chaos they had just caused. On the top of the ridge they had cleared minutes before, the first of the galloping horsemen appeared.

* * *

Eustace had left Fiona, Ally and Kita under guard when they reached the temple's main chamber. They looked around to see how much work had been done to clear the debris of the collapsed ceiling. An irregular hole let light in, which illuminated the uncovered dais. Framed by rubble like this, it was easy to imagine the stone slab being used for sacrifices. Dangling down from the opening, and winding in and out of darkness, was a rope ladder. Most of the rubble and earth had simply been moved to corners of the room. Picks, shovels and other tools were propped up against the wall. Kita was horrified by the destruction and Ally and Fiona hugged the distraught girl to comfort her.

The five soldiers stood arrayed around the slab, keeping their captives between their line and the rubble pile. Their sand coloured uniforms were dusty and untidy from the work of clearing the room. Ally found her mind wandering, and considered the cut of their uniforms. Her family was in the fashion business, and she couldn't help but occasionally mentally critique other people's clothing. The outfits were neatly cut, if obviously mass produced. They lacked any insignia to identify the troops, though Ally had deduced they were German based upon occasional words they exchanged.

Fiona, meanwhile, was studying what she could see of the walls. Rather than thinking about her imminent death, she wanted to find out more of the temples secrets. The section of hieroglyphs she chose to concentrate on was rather racy, and she found herself warming at thoughts of the activities described.

Thoughts of fashion or sex were cut short by the return of Eustace. The chinless Nazi buffoon looked even more ridiculous in his robes- a gaudy and overblown misinterpretation of a priest's attire. He swung the blade he'd stolen over his head. "I have my own ceremony devised. It would not do to channel power to these savages." He levelled the sword at Kita. This broke her out of her reverie and now Ally and Fiona had to hold her back. Eustace, all wrapped up in his supposed superiority, didn't even notice the glare she gave the sword tip. He continued, "It will be much better if the Fuhrer gets the power he deserves. And I deserve, as well, of course."

Eustace turned on his heel and walked to the slab. He rested the point of the sword on the surface and twirled it. He was about to start pontificating some more, but Ally was listening to something else, a familiar buzz. She leaned across to whisper to Fiona, "How do you feel about making a break for it?"

Fiona nodded toward the semi circle of soldiers who guarded them. "Oh, I think they will be otherwise engaged very soon." Ally reassured her.

Just as Eustace was about to start a monologue, a head and shoulders appeared in the daylight above them, casting its shadow over the slab. It shouted a warning in German. Eustace looked around, confused, until one of the troops translated in broken English, "There is a airplane. It approaches."

"Damnation! It must be that slut Jiggleswick. I thought I had put her out of operation. Shoot it down!" Eustace fumed. He waved the sword at the figure above, who shrugged. Eustace gestured at his ersatz translator, who shouted instructions. The shadow disappeared and soon after there was the crackling of gunfire overhead. "We must do this quickly. You two, bring me the girl! Quickly now! Schnell!"

The two troops nearest Ally, Fiona and Kita moved toward them, making the mistake of getting between them and the other three. When they were within arm's length there was the loud buzz of aero engines passing close by. All the troops looked up at the sound, and the gunfire that accompanied it. Ally moved quickly, pinning the nearest soldier's gun against his chest and punching him hard. She could land a mean blow when she wanted, and the troop started falling backwards. Kita moved quickly, producing a dagger from some secret hiding place and thrusting it into the second troop's chest.

Ally was familiar with shotguns and hunting rifles. The weapon she found in her hands was similar enough that she could turn it on the other troops and fire it. The one she missed dived for cover rather than fire back Ally kept the gun pointed at the rock he hid behind.

Fiona took decisive strides forward and kicked Eustace hard in the crotch. He doubled up, and she cracked her knee into his face, knocking him over. The comical robe fell open, revealing a surprisingly large, half-hard, cock. Fiona's eyes were wide. "What a waste." she commented after a moment.

There were three closely spaced explosions somewhere up above. Dust and stones rattled down, and the hiding soldier took the opportunity to make a break for the grand doors to the catacombs. He had hardly squeezed through the gap before another noise, a terrible rumbling crashing, came from the tunnels and drove him back. Hands held high in surrender, he ran back toward the dais.

Ally kept the soldier covered, "You're the one who speaks English!" she shouted.

"Yes!"

Whatever the noise from the tunnels was, it was growing too loud for speech. Ally signalled for him to come closer and checked him for weapons. She motioned for Fiona and Kita to climb the ladder ahead of her before starting up it one-handed, the gun slung clumsily over her shoulder. The scared soldier watched, but made no hostile moves. After Kita and Fiona had dragged Ally out of the hole, he ran to the bottom of the ladder and followed them.

Another three explosions shook the camp, but they were drowned out by the sound of rushing water hammering through the tunnels.

* * *

They had dragged the dead guard in from outside and tied the hands of the one Ginge had clobbered. Amid studied their machine pistols and claimed one for himself. He offered the other to Ginge, who shook his head, "A rifle is more my style, I'll stick with this." The gun went to the most senior of the men with them.

The thin German watched this activity with a detached gaze, aware that at least one armed man was watching at any time. Eventually Amid turned to him, "Who are you?"

"My name is Arnold." the thin man replied in his precise English.

"He's one of the raiders." Quince announced, "Takes his orders from Herr Hitler himself."

"That is interesting. I am sure we will have some questions for you later. Tie him up." Two of the men followed Amid's order. They found a short piece of rope in a pile of supplies. Arnold almost docilely allowed them to guide him to a chair, sit him in it and tie his hands behind his back.

While the German agent was being bound, Ginge walked away from the group. He peeped out of the tent flap and, when he was sure there was no-one else around, popped his head out. "I think we should be out there quickly." he announced when he came back in. "I can hear our kite heading this way. It's going to get interesting soon."

"Very well." Amid considered Arnold suspiciously, judging what to do with him.

"Leave me a weapon old chap. I'm in no state to run around the site with you young fellows." Quince offered. He neglected to mention that this was because he was horribly hung over from consuming most of Montana Smith's secret stash of bourbon the night before. He accepted a vintage rifle, and quickly proved he knew the way around it. When he was satisfied that it was fully working he laid it on the table pointing at Arnold.

They exited through the door flap at the rear of the tent and gathered the two point men they had left outside. Keeping low, they skirted the edge of the site until they found a spoil pile which would make a good vantage point. By now, the Hooligan was being fired on by soldiers. Ginge was surprised to see little spits of flame from the Hooligan's windows as people on board returned fire.

Picking targets from the nearest group of soldiers, the squad settled in against the rubble and started firing at them. Some of them fell, but the rest didn't seem to notice. After a few more volleys they began to work out that they were under fire from someone other than the plane- which was now at the far side of the dig site- but there were too few of them to do anything about it, so they scattered. There was a huge explosion in amongst the vehicles on the far side of the dig, and they scattered in different directions.

Despite the chaos, the five men on the ridge had yet to have anyone come in range of their guns, so they stood and started moving toward the battle. It was a fatal move, as a heavy machine gun behind a group of tents opened up and cut them all down. The Hooligan had come around for another pass, and the heavy gun turned on it. Taking hits, and with an engine now trailing smoke, the plane banked away again and started a run for safety.

The Hooligan disappeared behind the screening smoke from the burning vehicles, and the chatter of the heavy machine gun stopped. There were another three explosions from near the trucks. The remaining troops had all taken cover, some aiming toward the tents, unsure where the shots had been coming from, others pointing in the direction the plane had come from. Amid checked to see what had their attention and saw a rag-tag cavalry of horses and camels charging over the nearest ridge line. Every so often, one of the riders would wheel his steed as it crested the rise, framed against the sky.

The riders had a large open space, and then another rise, to cross before they reached the site. If the heavy machine gun could get into position, that last uphill stretch could be carnage. Amid was considering tactics and ways to intercept the gun when Ginge tapped him on the shoulder and pointed toward the main trench of the dig. Three figures in simple white robes had clambered out of the hole, looked around and then dived behind some rubble for cover. "That was Ally and Fiona. It must have been Kita with them." Another figure, dressed in soldier's uniform, appeared from the hole. He chose his own rubble pile and hid behind it.

As the rest of the squad took carefully aimed shots at the troops below them, Amid and Ginge considered ways to get a shot at the machine gunners. They traced the site's paths back to where they thought the shots had come from. To get shots at the rapidly approaching cavalry, they would have to schlep the weapon past the main trench and the rubble pile where Ally was crouched with a machine pistol. Perhaps they wouldn't have to move, and could do their best work where they were.

As Amid and Ginge set their sights on the nearest group of troops there was another noise. It started as a roaring whistle, getting deeper as it grew louder.. A spout of dust and debris shot up out of the main trench. As the first of the pebbles and rocks began to rain down, the noise became a thunder.

✳ ✳ ✳

Fiona had spotted the four men coming down the path with ammunition boxes and what appeared to be a piece of tubing. Ally recognised the machine gun and rightly guessed that it would not bode well for it to be set up. She popped the magazine from her machine pistol and checked how many rounds were in it. There weren't many. She could possibly bring down some of the machine gun crew, perhaps that would be enough, but then they would be trapped and unarmed.

Kita, however, had spotted a downed troop, with magazines scattered around his body. She started crawling toward him, looking even more cat like than ever. Just as she clasped a pair of magazines and prepared to pass them back, she froze.

The three of them could feel the ground they lay on shaking. The vibration rapidly gave way to something else- a whooshing whistle as air was pushed out of the temple. The rush of air though the narrow gap was such that it lifted sand and stones and tossed them high.

Mesmerised by the tower of dirt rising from the main trench, the crew of the heavy machine gun stared past Ally and Fiona, not registering them in the slightest. Their eyes followed the dust spout to its zenith and their mouths fell open.

"Run!" Fiona suggested loudly. Ally and Kita could see the logic of the cry. They ran along the trench side of the spoil pile, then rounded it and charged up the path the heavy machine gun had come down.

The sound of rushing air ceased, only to be replaced by another, more terrifying noise as water boiled up from the ground.

* * *

Eustace was roused by the rumble of the floor underneath him and the rush of air over and around him. "Bitch!" he pronounced as he remembered how he came to be in his current predicament.

The dust obscured the illumination from the ceiling, but there was still enough light to see the four dead troops lying around the altar. He wiped away the blood from his broken nose, cursed Fiona some more, and tried to stand. The floor moved and bounced under his hands and feet, and it was harder than he had expected.

Eustace rolled over, pushed himself up with his hands and scrabbled his feet along the floor until he was upright. He stumbled and crawled his way up to the slab and then around to the bottom of the rope ladder. His robe whipped and snapped about him, making it hard to catch the rungs. He twisted and tugged at it until it flew away and twirled up and out of the hole. Now he stood naked by the rope ladder, battered and scoured by the stones and sand rushing out of the tunnel.

Boosting off the stone slab, Eustace started climbing the ladder, hand over strenuous hand. With the wind flowing around him and the dust bringing tears to his eyes he couldn't always see where the next rung was and swung his hands around reaching for it. Suddenly, the battering stopped.

Eustace swung back and forth, clinging tight to the rope. He dared to open his eyes and looked down. What seemed like a long way away, the floor moved below him. Wedged in the grand doors to the tunnel network was a boat. Water was flowing around it, but the way it was quivering it was obviously about to push through. As he blocked the opening, only the groans of shifting stones and flexing wood gave any indication of what was happening below.

Eustace scrabbled for the lip of the hole, desperate to pull himself out as fast as he could.

It was far too late. The prow of the boat suddenly appeared, illuminated by the sunlight filtering around Eustace's body, and bore toward him in judgement.

* * *

With a rending and tearing, and the crack of shattering stone, the remnants of the boat were pushed high in the air atop a foaming spout of water. All eyes in and around the dig site turned to the incredible sight.

Eustace was a terrified figurehead, pinned to the prow of the boat- the only part still recognisable. He was probably screaming, but no-one could hear anything over the thunder of the water. The spout rose and rose, tossing out debris, and eventually discarding Eustace and his craft, before finally topping out.

Fiona dragged Ally and Kita off the path and into cover behind a rubble pile just in time to avoid a volley of falling rocks as large as her head. They held each other tight as possible as smaller stones, planking and splinters fell around their hiding place. The painful, pattering debris was followed by water that hit them like a punch and soaked them instantly.

Elsewhere around the site, soldiers were felled by the stones and planks cascading from the water spout. Others dropped their weapons and ran, preferring to test the mercy of the charging cavalry or Amid's squad rather than be pummelled by debris. A couple were unlucky enough to be cut down before their attackers understood they were surrendering, but most of them were spared.

* * *

Arnold and Quince both listened to the gunfire outside and wondered how the fight was progressing. Quince adjusted the rifle on the table. "It must feel terrible to have the tables turn so quickly." he opined.

"The battle is not yet over." Arnold pointed out. "But even if that fool assistant of yours doesn't prevail I think I shall be happy."

"How so? We shall simply turn you over to the authorities."

"I will simply end up in jail. It will be safer than what is coming."

"And if, God forbid, Eustace succeeds?"

"Then I shall go back to the Fatherland and be given another mission in another part of the globe." Arnold was considering his next comment very carefully. He decided he might as well continue, "Perhaps one day I shall disappear. Espionage and intrigue are games for young men. And as you grow older you collect more.... secrets which can get you killed. I started with some deadly secrets of my own even before I began to learn those of others."

"Do tell. We have nothing to do but talk until the battle is over."

"There are certain.... types of people the regime does not approve of. I am not a Jew as your brother-in-law is, but I have particular..... desires."

"Oh, you're one of those chaps who likes chaps. I know a few of them. But then, I'm in academia, that sort of thing happens. I hadn't realised they were a problem for Hitler and his type. I thought that was what drove them, what with all the uniforms and dressing up and discipline and such."

Arnold didn't get a chance to answer. The ground beneath their feet grumbled as something down the hill shifted. They noticed that the sounds of shooting and explosions had ceased, replaced by a whooshing and whistling then a powerful rumble.

They stared in the direction of the commotion, even though all they could see was the flap of the door. Suddenly, however, the tent wall was rushing toward them. It tore apart and revealed a large, tumbling piece of timber. The section of decking ploughed through the middle of the tent, demolishing the table between Arnold and Quince and sending them both flying.

Arnold found himself lying on the floor, staring at the ceiling of the tent. He moved his legs around, testing them to see if they were still there, and his arms as best he could. Satisfied nothing was broken, he sat up. Across the floor, Quince obviously hadn't fared as well. The angle of his right shin told Arnold that the Professor's leg was broken. Quince looked more dazed than anything else, shocked at the sudden violence visited upon him by a random piece of woodwork.

Shuffling around, Arnold found a piece of shattered wood from the table. The edge was serrated and just sharp enough to saw through the rope that held his wrists. He left a few splinters in his palms, but soon the rope frayed and parted.

Quince's rifle was close to the hole in the rear wall of the tent where the tumbling timber had torn its way out. It was bent into a U, far beyond usefulness. Arnold decided he wouldn't need it, it was better to leave. But then he looked down at Quince, who was pale and about to pass out. The spy couldn't just leave the academic like that. His chair had shattered as he fell over. He picked up the arms and placed them either side of Quince's damaged lower leg.

"This will hurt." Arnold announced, matter-of-factly, before straightening Quince's leg. The Professor didn't scream, he simply passed out. Arnold used the rope he had been tied with to lash the splints around Quince's leg. Satisfied they were secure, he kissed Quince on the cheek then walked briskly out the back of the tent.

* * *

The spout showed no immediate sign of subsiding, and it kept throwing occasional chunks of history into the air, though few went as far as the boat and initial barrage. Amid and Ginge walked some of the way down the hill to the main trench, stopping well short of the falling water and stones. "Well, that was unexpected." Ginge commented.

"It has been said that some day the waters of the valley would flow again, when they are most needed. If Miss Jiggleswick caused this, perhaps she is referred to in the ancients' writings. I should study them."

"Do you really believe all that guff?"

Amid reddened, "Well, of course not. Not as a rule. But these last few days have certainly been something special. I thought perhaps Fiona was to be the One."

"The One?"

"If we had the chance we were to enact the rituals one last time, and find a maidenhood to sacrifice."

"Sacrifice? Surely you don't mean to kill someone?"

"NO! Oh no, not at all. The maiden sacrifices her maidenhood, if that makes sense. The maiden opens herself up to the possibility of fertility. She..... blooms, and experiences something new. In doing so, she embodies the hopes and spirit of her people, all the inhabitants of the valley."

Ginge couldn't stifle his laugh, "I'm afraid you're far off base if you want Jiggles to give up her virtue. She did that many years ago. Under a haystack with a chap called Roger, so she says. Fiona is the one you need for maidenhood, depending upon what she and Ally have been up to since we last saw them."

As if responding to the calling of her name by Ginge, Fiona appeared, along with Ally and Kita. They were skirting the haze of water around the spout, but were already soaked and coated in mud. Ally grinned when she spotted Ginge and Amid and started jogging toward them. She wrapped her arms around Ginge in a muddy hug.

"Good lord, who gave you a rifle? You're positively dangerous with one of those."

Kita hugged Amid and started explaining everything that had happened to the girls. "We have had something of an adventure." Ally offered as a shorter version.

"That fool Eustace wanted to kill me." Fiona added angrily. She had decided the dress she wore was far too dirty and shrugged out of it. The fact that she was standing naked in full view not just of her friends but also the captured troops, Amid's squad and the cavalry bothered her not one jot. She had come a long,

long way from the demure, almost terrified young flower they had flown into Africa. "I tried to explain that it's not about death, but about sex, but he would not listen. Did anyone see where he landed?"

Amid had laid a hand on Kita's arm to gently halt the flow of her narrative. He nodded to where Fiona stood, her smooth pale skin and lovely conical breasts streaked with mud, looking every inch the goddess. Sensing their attention, she turned toward them. Kita applauded the full frontal view. Amid drew himself up to stand straight and as tall as he could, and dusted himself down as best he could. "Miss.... erm, Fiona, I would like very much to discuss the sex rites of the temple with you. And, if you wish, there may be a very important role for you to play in them."

***

Jiggles managed to put the Hooligan down with the minimum of drama, coming to a halt by the ribbon of compacted dirt that passed for the road to the dig site. From here they could just see the top of the water spout that had erupted from the main trench. Uncertain what they might find, the plane taxied up the track as fast as it could on one engine. When the site came into view, they stared, uncomprehending, at the chaos that was revealed.

One of the gunners in the Hooligan was dead and two were injured. They laid the dead one out respectfully in the shadow of the plane and carried the injured ones toward the fountain. Cavalry on horse and camel back spotted them and galloped over. After a quick discussion with Yusuf, they took the injured men and rushed them away to be treated.

They skirted the rim of the natural bowl that held the dig site, which was now filling up and forming its own little lake, until they spotted Amid and Ginge and a busy group of priestesses. Drawing closer, they could see that the priestesses were fussing over three naked women. It wasn't until they were practically beside the group that they realised who the nymphs were.

"Jiggles!" Ally cried out, squeezing out of the crush to hug her friend, "Was that you dropping explosives everywhere?"

"It was. The kite got a little shot up, though. Whatever is going on here?"

Ally took Jiggles and Montana's arms and walked them closer to the throng. "Well, you see, Amid and the priestesses are going to do one of the old-style sacrifice ceremonies, and Fiona is the star of the show."

"Their sacrificing Fiona?" Montana asked.

"Not Fiona, her virginity. It's all about sex in the valley, it represents all the positive things about life. All that stuff. Well, when everything has been tidied up we are going to set up a temporary temple and do the ceremony."

"That does sound interesting." Montana admitted. He was trying very hard not to stare at Ally's naked, and still mud-streaked, body as she talked. Her nipples, atop those perfect spherical breasts, had peaked up and she was obviously excited. "Quince will be most interested in this. He'll want to take notes and everything."

"Where is the Professor?" Jiggles asked, realising someone was missing from the crowd.

Ally's smile only faltered slightly, "Ah, we found him in the main tent after the battle. He'd broken his leg. He had been guarding one of the leaders of the Germans, a chap called Arnold who can't be found anywhere. Strange thing is, this Arnold put the Prof's leg in splints before he left, and old Quince was muttering something about him being a decent chap really."

"Strange. I shall go and talk to him, see what he can tell me about this Arnold fellow. I have contacts in the Government who may be interested in him. I'll meet you all later and you can tell me all about the ceremony." Montana gave a little bow and wandered off to talk, first, to Amid and Ginge.

"Amid and Ginge think that you probably did this." Ally pointed at the water spout and its ever growing lake.

"Yes, I think we may have. Not that I'm complaining, darling, but what happened to your clothes?"

Ally glanced down at her body and giggled, "I had forgotten I'd taken them off. The priestesses are going to find us something to wear. Come and meet Kita, she's adorable."

* * *

The lake filled quickly, flooding the other trenches before anything could be done to rescue the artefacts in them. The high tide mark crept up and up, but never really threatened what was left of the tents. Eventually, the water found one of Amid's secret tunnels and flowed through it and out into the dry ravines. As it scoured the inside of the tunnel wider, eventually a whole section of the ridge collapsed and yet another wave flooded down the valley as the resurgent river continued its journey.

The water re-wrote the map of the valley, jumping from long dead river beds across open spaces and around rocks and structures. It washed away stretches of the road and caused chaos when it rushed out of the valley. This was what drew the authorities to the dig site before the radio could be repaired or a messenger sent to the nearest town.

So it was that the grand ceremony didn't happen as soon as hoped. Professor Quince appreciated this, as it meant that he could be flown out with the other injured men- after Ginge had worked his magic on the Hooligan using parts salvaged from broken trucks- and returned before he could miss anything.

The receding waters of the lake revealed a treasure trove of statuary and other relics, washed out of the tunnels by the extreme force of the deluge flowing through them, and an aerial survey of the great lake at the head of the valley showed that structures had been revealed by the water which had drained from it. Montana set to cataloguing the riches at the dig site whilst Amid and Sorya commandeered the returning workers and archaeology students to arrange an al fresco version of the temple chamber. The most important find was the grand stone slab of the altar, which everything else was moved to frame.

It was over a week before the authorities stopped visiting and asking questions. Even then, they only had four days before delegations from the British and American embassies were due to arrive with government officials to view the discoveries.

On the first free day Amid, Kita and Sorya explained the history of the Valley of the Wizards, the knowledge which gave it its power and the sex rites which had developed and been passed down the years as part of their culture.

Montana, Quince and Fiona took copious notes and were regularly joined by any number of people who had suddenly developed an interest in social history. By the end of the day long session, Fiona was a familiar shade of red. Now, however, it was the heat of excitement rather than embarrassment.

The next morning Sorya led a blessing service over the graves of everyone who had died in the battle for the dig site. Regardless of whether they had been marauding German or defending local, when a body had been found it had been laid to rest respectfully in the next available grave. Even Eustace, found crushed under boat remnants, had been afforded some dignity in death.

The solemn duties dispensed with, everyone retired to tents to prepare for the night's activities. Kita had joined Ally, Fiona and Jiggles in their tent and had made for herself a nest of cushions in one corner. She stretched across them to take tea, but sprang up and was jumping around as soon as they finished. Fiona moved toward the spot Kita pointed her at and stood, nervous with anticipation. None of the shyness she had displayed when they first arrived remained. Kita asked a question and Fiona smiled and nodded.

Fiona was wearing one of her shapeless one-piece overalls. They were very practical for working in an archaeology trench, but could be more flattering. Kita popped a few buttons and the baggy outfit dropped to the floor, leaving her in knickers and a blouse. Jiggles and Ally moved in to help pop the little mother-of-pearl buttons through their holes and then remove her blouse. Ally deftly released Fiona's brassiere and tossed it aside.

Kita knelt before Fiona and reached up to slide her fingers under the band of her knickers and slowly pull them down. When Fiona stepped out of the underwear, Kita reached up to play her fingers through the springy pubic hair that had been revealed. Staring up at Fiona, Kita asked a question. Fiona considered the request, then nodded and replied. Kita grinned. She went over to a bag she had put her necessities in and started going through it.

"What did she ask?" Jiggles wondered aloud.

"Kita wanted to know if I would like to be shaved."

"Really? That sounds interesting."

"Well, it is how all of the statues are portrayed, so it seems appropriate." Ally grinned. Her fingers had been teasing at the cone of Fiona's left breast, working the nipple up to a stiffened point. Fiona shivered with excitement.

Kita brought over a cut-throat razor and shaving kit. "From Amid." she announced.

"I see you have been planning." Ally told Kita, who seemed to understand. Turning to Fiona, Ally added, "I hear that Amid is the, er, Master of Ceremonies, or whatever the appropriate name is for it. If what Ginge has told me is true, then you are a very lucky lady."

Fiona flushed, a mix of excitement and embarrassment. "I think, before we go any further, I would be more comfortable if you three were naked as well." she announced with a smirk.

Ally, Jiggles and Kita complied eagerly, and dis-robed quickly. When there wasn't a stitch of clothing on any of them they guided Fiona to one of the canvas chairs. Under guidance, she shuffled forward until her buttock cheeks balanced on the edge of the seat, then she leant back. With her feet flat on the floor she spread her legs, letting Kita shuffle between them and nestle close with the razor.

They had brought a bowl of hot water in with them. Jiggles tested the temperature, then took the shaving kit and worked up a lather. All the while, Ally was stood behind Fiona, leaning over her and playing with her nipples. Much as she loved the teasing, Fiona reached up and clasped Ally's wrists. "Best if you stop that. I don't want to be quivering when Kita's waving that blade about." Ally gave Fiona a kiss and backed off to watch.

Jiggles used the brush to spoon the lather onto Fiona's bush and then rubbed it in to the hair. Fiona bit her bottom lip and closed her eyes, trying not to move under Jiggles' fingers. When the hand and brush stopped working at her hair, she opened an eye to look down. She closed it again, quickly, when she saw Kita carefully placing the blade of the razor by the foam around her pubes.

Kita carefully angled the blade and gently touched it to Fiona's skin. She drew it down slowly, snipping the hairs cleanly. After a half inch stroke, Kita lifted the razor and cleaned it on a towel Ally held out. She brought the blade back again for another half inch stroke.

Slowly and carefully, Kita removed Fiona's hair. Each swipe of the blade uncovered pale pink skin. Eventually almost all the lather, and the hair it was worked into, had been removed by the sharp straight blade. Kita took another towel from Ally and used it to gently clean the area just above Fiona's now deep red and puffy pussy lips. She ran her finger tips over the revealed skin, searching for any hairs she had missed. Before she could tidy them up, Ally and Jiggles tested Fiona's newly shaved skin for themselves. They pushed harder than Kita, moving the sheath over her clitoris and eliciting a moan. Kita appreciated the effect, but, with a grin, she waved them off with the razor.

With light, deft strokes, Kita shaved off the last little bits of hair she had missed in the first pass. After cleaning the area again, she planted a kiss on the clitoral hood and muttered a little blessing ahead of the evening's events. She waved Ally and Jiggles in to offer their own devotions. Ally stole the chance to sneak a taste from between Fiona's puffed up fanny lips. Fiona rested her hands on Ally's head, wanting to urge her to lick some more, but Kita tutted and told her off. "It seems my next orgasm must be provided by Amid " Fiona sighed.

"I do like the look of your pussy without any hair." Jiggles commented. "It really draws your attention down to the cleft. I think I would like to have my hair shaved."

"Let's all do it." Ally suggested. "I'll go first." She helped Fiona out of her seat and took her place. With a cheeky grin, Fiona took the razor from Kita and prepared to wield it.

When they were all shaved, there were four simple dresses for them to wear, simple shifts with only a few buttons holding them up. Fiona's was a pure white, whilst the others were a pale blue. Attired in these simple pieces of cotton, they left the tent when the sun was low in the sky and the heat of the day was no longer so oppressive.

There was a crowd forming. Many of the workers had returned, Mustafa's caravan had detoured to the site for the celebrations and to have a look around, and the priests and priestesses of Sorya and Amid's sect were there to officiate, all wearing their animal head masks. They all stepped aside to let Fiona, Ally, Jiggles and Kita through, occasionally applauding them.

The stone slab that was the centrepiece of the improvised temple had come to rest halfway up the slope from the shore of the brand new lake. The statues had been arrayed around the slab in a semi circle, with the larger ones at the top of the slope and nearest the stone. The figures formed a barrier beyond which the spectators didn't venture. Kita, Jiggles and Ally crossed the threshold and joined a gaggle of priestesses who, with Montana and Quince, were watching from a privileged position. Fiona was met by Sorya- wearing her hawk's head mask and a simple white slip- who led her up to the slab.

There had been a buzz of conversation, but now that Fiona stood beside the slab it ceased and the site was silent. Sorya turned Fiona to face the crowd and they bowed. Fiona stared out at all the people who were there to watch her and felt strangely elated and excited. A few weeks before, she would have been horrified at the thought of what was about to happen, but that timid girl was no more. She felt a throb from her denuded genitals and a warmth that spread out from her groin.

Sorya plucked at the buttons of Fiona's slip and it floated down to the ground. When Sorya stepped aside, Fiona's slim, pale body practically shone in the evening light. There was a moment's awed silence then applause, which seemed out of place for a religious ceremony but made Fiona beam with pride. The crowd went silent again, before parting to let Amid and Ginge- each wearing only a loin cloth- through. The two men strolled up the hill, Amid giving every impression he belonged there, and Ginge bumbling alongside trying to stay in step.

Ginge stopped beside Sorya, but Amid stepped in front of Fiona and bowed to her. He took her hands, "Are you ready for the ceremony?" She smiled and nodded.

At a signal from Sorya, Ginge stepped up behind Amid and tugged at the two strings that fastened his loin cloth. When he pulled the strip of fabric away, Amid was revealed in all his glory to Fiona. No-one else could see what she saw, but the happy O of her mouth told them all they needed to know. Amid lifted Fiona's chin so he could kiss her. "Thank you for blessing us." he told her.

Amid was supposed to guide Fiona onto the stone for the next, obvious, step in the ceremony. She, however, had a different idea. Turning him around so that the congregation could see his magnificent, stiff and gently curving penis, she dropped to her knees before him. This was not a part of the standard ceremony, but one of the rules was that it was open to improvisation.

Fiona's first view of an erect penis- any penis- had been Eustace's in the temple. This was much more intimate, and far more pleasurable, though she hadn't the slightest clue what to do next. The crowd was hushed, expectant. Fiona had her palms flat on the outsides of his thighs and her face close to his gently twitching, rock hard erection. She drew her hands around and leaned in closer. The bobbing hard on tapped the tip of her nose and she nearly broke the mood by giggling. With great self control, she kept the laughter in her throat and pecked a kiss just below the head of Amid's cock. She liked the feel of the skin on her lips, and started nibbling with them, up and down the shaft. Meanwhile, her hands had come around and she held a testicle gently between the thumb and forefinger of each hand.

Emboldened, Fiona's tongue sneaked out and she licked from tip to base. The whole crowd sighed with pleasure at the sight, so she licked back up the shaft and pursed her lips over the head. Amid held himself still, with just a quiver in his muscles betraying the emotions he felt. He may have been acting as the priest, but it was always the maiden who directed the ceremony, her desires were paramount. And when her desires were to slowly take the length of his erection into her mouth, he wasn't going to complain.

Fiona backed off from Amid's erection and licked her lips. She worked up saliva and dipped back, taking the whole of the head into her mouth in one quick, brave move. She held the head with her lips, licking it and then sucking it like a lollipop. Amid shivered, his self control tested by Fiona's tongue. She may not have had any experience, but she had enthusiasm and imagination.

Fiona released Amid's cock head. She wasn't sure how close he was and she wanted him to come inside her pussy rather than her mouth. She stood, and gave Amid's saliva soaked penis a loving look before glancing back at the slab. Amid helped her onto the stone. She swung her legs around and stretched out along its length then beckoned Amid toward her. When he was close enough, she reached down and whirled her fingers around the slippery slick erection.

Amid bent forward and kissed Fiona's breasts. She relinquished control of his manhood for a while and let him explore her body with his lips, tongue and fingers. As delicate digits teased at her recently shaved mons and lips nibbled under her chin and up to her mouth, she held her hands over her head and resisted the temptation to guide him.

As Amid and Fiona kissed, his fingers slipped around her pussy lips then sneaked between them. Fiona drew her knees up and spread her legs, urging him into her. When their lips parted, she told Amid, "I'm ready." Amid nodded and moved around to the end of the slab. Kissing the insides of her calves and thighs as he went, he worked his way up Fiona's body. He paid particular attention to her clitoris, teasing around it and sucking it into his mouth.

Fiona's climax was growing as Amid pressed the flat of his tongue against her clit and then licked up and down her lips. Before she tipped over the edge,

Amid stopped and carried on his lips' trip up her body. He kissed around her navel and then up toward her breasts. When he reached her lips they kissed passionately as the head of Amid's glorious erection lodged between the wet and ready lips of Fiona's pussy.

Fiona was surprised at the feel of a man inside her, even if it was only just there. Eager for the full length, she reached down to grasp his cheeks and pulled him toward her. There was none of the pain she had expected, just a sudden and exciting feeling of being filled. Her tongue thrust into Amid's mouth and played around as she reached back up and grasped his hair. As Fiona wrapped her legs around Amid, the crowd erupted in applause. Neither of them noticed.

Amid pulled out a short way, the pressure of Fiona's legs holding him in place stopped him moving too far. Then he pushed back in, grinding his pubic bone against her mons and clitoris. Fiona decided she really liked the sensations of Amid moving inside her, so she lowered her legs to let him move more freely. They stared into each others eyes as he moved and her climax drew closer.

Amid and Fiona paused in their love making, suddenly intrigued to see what was going on around them. Except that, at first, they saw something else. They both saw the old temple, the one now under water, in its glory days. Priests and priestesses were all around them, naked but for their bird head masks. Some of them were watching, whilst others were having ceremonies of their own. The couplings- and triplings, quadlings and more- were of almost every possible combination. "They are doing that in your honour." Amid declared.

The vision cleared, and they were back in the new, open air, incarnation of the temple. Some details were the same. There was an orgy going on. Nearest to them, Ginge was cross-legged on the ground before the slab, with Sorya- still wearing her mask but nothing else- in his lap, impaled upon little Ginge. There were far too many other details that they couldn't see, but that didn't matter to Amid or Fiona. They went back to making love.

As Fiona and Amid had mounted the slab, Jiggles had felt her slip fall from her body. She didn't know who in the crowd around her had unbuttoned it, and didn't care. Everyone else was naked or stripping and she was surrounded by bosoms, bottoms and hard ons. She turned to Montana, to see he was only wearing his boots and holding up a familiar jug of lubricating oil. "Would you do me the honour of allowing me to bugger you?" he asked jokily.

"Why, of course." Jiggles took hold of his erection and led him to one of the statues she had spotted earlier. It depicted an elephant and was low and wide, topping out at waist height. Letting go of Montana, she leaned over the carved animal, her nipples rubbing sensually on the polished stone surface. Montana poured oil on the small of her back, just above the swell of her buttocks. It found the cleft between her cheeks and ran down it, to be caught by one of Montana's fingers and swirled around the puckered entrance of her arsehole.

Montana pushed one, then another, finger into Jiggles' behind, working lubricant in and getting her more and more excited. They had an audience, three of the archaeology students had their trousers around their ankles and were stroking their erections. Jiggles beckoned them over, then chose one to come closer, so that she could get her lips around the head of his cock to lick and tease it. Just as she got him into her mouth, Montana removed his fingers and slid his glorious hard on into her behind.

Ally and Kita had been learning bits of each other's languages, but when they faced each other in the erotic heat of the excited crowd, they didn't have to say anything. They each reached out and undid the other's dress. When they were both naked, they kissed and caressed. Ally ground her bald mons against Kita's and could feel the warmth rising from the other woman's pussy.

Kita pulled away from Ally's lips just long enough to point to a piece of flat ground a short way up the slope. Ally nodded and they skipped quickly over to the space. Kita lay down and Ally straddled her head. As Kita's tongue teased at her wrinkled lips and worked up toward her clitoris, Ally leaned forward so her face was between Kita's thighs. She kissed and licked at the puffy lips, then placed her mouth over the prominent clitoris and sucked hard.

Professor Quince had been content to sit in his chair, broken leg straight out in front of him, and watch the orgy develop from his vantage point. So he was surprised when he found a young man and woman standing naked before him. They were both gorgeous. The man was slim, but with well defined muscles, and sported a glorious erection. The woman was tall, with an hour glass figure and large but firm breasts. They both looked down at the Professor, smiling, and he realised what they were silently asking. With an apologetic look at the man, he pointed at the woman.

The naked man bowed to Quince and took a step back. The woman stepped forward and knelt down between the Professor's legs. Careful of his wounded limb, she unfastened his trousers and reverently drew out his erection. The woman's dark hair fell around her face and obscured her first kiss of his penis. She paused and drew the black strands aside so that he could watch her take his hard on into her mouth and slowly work her lips down it. "Oh, I say." Quince sighed.

Lalya had been grinding her full buttocks against her husband-to-be's crotch as the sexual excitement grew. Now, as so many others let their passions take hold, she wanted to act on her desires. She took Yusuf's hand and led him over to the nearest statue. The naked, hawk-headed woman was nearly one and a half times Lalya's size, standing with hands behind her back and breasts arched up and prominent. Lalya studied the pose, then made her husband stand back as she stripped. When she was naked, she stood on one of the statue's feet and mimicked the pose.

Yusuf dropped to his knees before Lalya. He kissed her toes and feet and his hands worked their way up from her ankles to her knees. At his gentle suggestion, Lalya spread her legs, planting one foot on each of the statue's. Yusuf's fingers teased the inside of her thighs and his lips and tongue followed them. She placed her hands on his head and urged him to work his way up faster, leaning back against the statue and spreading her thighs some more. Yusuf's tongue sneaked between her pussy lips and she clasped him more tightly and pushed his face harder into her crotch.

Mustafa watched his son being led away and grinned. He liked his future daughter-in-law, she had a spirit that would buoy up his son's ambitions and help him live up to his potential. Hands touched Mustafa's shoulders and he turned to find the four young ladies who were travelling with his caravan. They were all naked, displaying their many charms to him. Eager hands reached out and started undressing him. He let his clothes be removed and savoured gentle hands, kisses and, eventually, warm lips around the head of his erection.

Fiona knew she was close. She could feel the beautiful pressure building inside her. To urge Amid on she started rocking her hips in time to his movements. He responded by thrusting harder and faster, lifting her buttocks off the stone. Fiona's hands clasped at Amid's shoulders and she moaned and cried in his ear as her climax approached.

The high pitched cry of Fiona's orgasm was lost in the ecstatic noises of the orgy. The only other people who noticed were Sorya and Ginge, and they went back to their lovemaking almost immediately.

Amid had yet to come. He was still moving in Fiona, keeping her on a plateau of pleasure. She wanted to help him, but found the constant exquisite joy of a rolling orgasm meant she could hardly move. Amid's thrusts grew faster and faster, until, with one last push, he came deep inside Fiona.

As they both floated down from their climaxes, Fiona and Amid watched the debauchery going on around them. "That is all for you." Amid said again.

"I am honoured." Fiona replied breathlessly.

Sorya arched her back and placed her hands flat on the ground. Her mask fell off to reveal the ecstasy on her face as she, too, cried out her orgasm. Ginge leaned forward to suck at her prominent nipples.

Amid had slid out of Fiona to let her roll onto her side and watch Ginge and the priestess. She could feel his hard on bobbing against her thigh as he became excited by the sight of his step-cousin's joy. Eyeing the resurgent erection, Fiona asked, "Are you ready for some more? I would like to try a different position."

"Of course." Amid let Fiona roll over onto her front and raise her buttocks, presenting her pouting pussy to him. He guided himself into her, then grasped her waist as he began thrusting.

* * *

The orgy went on until sunrise the following day, and they were still finding discarded clothing the following week. Within a couple of days, the site was working again, almost as well as it had been before the raid and the flood. The statues in the impromptu temple were the first things the archaeology students started work on, with Sorya and Kita giving them advice on where they had originally been in the tunnels.

Ally and Fiona disappeared for a day into their tent and emerged with a completely re-worked, and far more flattering, wardrobe for Fiona. She walked taller and with far more confidence than when they had arrived. When a photographer for the British newspapers arrived to shoot the dig, he wanted her in as many pictures as possible.

Mustafa and his caravan of precious stones and ladies of easy virtue left, running a few days behind schedule, but he promised invitations to his son's wedding to all and sundry.

All the while, the Hooligan was flying back and forth, carrying dignitaries and equipment. Between trips, Ginge worked his magic to bring the plane back up to its normal standard. Between flights, and whilst he awaited certain key components, Sorya kept him busy. She had decided that she would very much like a copper haired child and took as many chances as their timetables allowed to try to conceive one.

Jiggles flew a team up to the head of the valley, to examine the structures revealed when the large lake there had drained. She took a tent and spent an eye-opening night with Montana and one of the students they had met during the ceremony.

Nearly two months after first flying in Professor Quince, Fiona and Eustace, the crew from Jiggleswick Air were ready to set off back to England. Quince, getting around on crutches now, had hobbled out to the runway to oversee the loading of various boxes full of items to wow his colleagues in London. Fiona, Kita, Amid, Montana and Sorya were all there as well, with gifts and requests for gifts to be sent back.

There were hugs and kisses all around, but everything that needed to be said had already been said, and the flight was going to be a long one. So Jiggles, Ally and Ginge climbed into the Hooligan and started pre-flight checks as the others backed off. The engines coughed into life and the plane taxied to the end of the runway. With final waves all round, Jiggles throttled up the engines and released the brakes. The plane bumped along the strip, gaining speed until it lifted off the ground and pulled up into the sky.

The Hooligan banked around for a pass over the airfield, waggling its wings to the crowd below. They followed the new river down the valley before climbing to cruising height. A new bridge was being built where the road had washed away, and the valley was changing in other ways. Where water had soaked the parched ground the earth was turning green, as long dormant grass sprouted. The mechanism Montana and Jiggles had tripped in the strange chamber under the lake had washed away, its exact workings a secret lost to the ages. The truth of how water came to flow down the Valley of the Wizards once more would also be lost to posterity- the story of the young English woman who gave her maidenhood in the traditional way was a far better narrative.

"We certainly left our mark, didn't we." Ginge commented wistfully.

"Indeed we did." Jiggles smiled.

"Did you hear what they've started calling this river?" Ally asked. "The Fiona."

"You could do a lot worse than having a river named after you." Jiggles decided.

Below them, the river started branching and meandering as it reached the flatter plain at the bottom of the valley. Jiggles pulled back on the stick and the Hooligan climbed into the perfect blue sky.

Don't miss out!

Visit the website below and you can sign up to receive emails whenever Mary Tales publishes a new book. There's no charge and no obligation.

https://books2read.com/r/B-A-XESE-JTQO

BOOKS2READ

Connecting independent readers to independent writers.

Also by Mary Tales

Jiggles
Jiggles and the Test Pilot
Jiggles and the Archaeologists
Jiggles and the Flying Boats

Love By The Book
Love By The Book
Love The Weekend

Mary Tales Collections
Mary Tales Omnibus
Contact Adventures
Contact Adventures 2 - First Timers
Cassie Gets it On
The Adventures of Jiggles

Meet The Gang
Meet The Gang

www.ingramcontent.com/pod-product-compliance
Lightning Source LLC
Chambersburg PA
CBHW071322130726
47996CB00002B/582